MAKING A JEWEL

CARVER LITERARY ARTS SOCIETY POETRIES, SHORT STORIES AND ESSAYS

ANTOINETTE FRANKLIN

AuthorHouse™
1663 Liberty Drive
Bloomington, IN 47403
www.authorhouse.com
Phone: 833-262-8899

Because of the dynamic nature of the Internet, any web addresses or links contained in this book may have changed since publication and may no longer be valid. The views expressed in this work are solely those of the author and do not necessarily reflect the views of the publisher, and the publisher hereby disclaims any responsibility for them.

Any people depicted in stock imagery provided by Getty Images are models, and such images are being used for illustrative purposes only.
Certain stock imagery © Getty Images.

This book is printed on acid-free paper.

ISBN: 978-1-6655-2294-6 (sc)
ISBN: 978-1-6655-2295-3 (e)

Print information available on the last page.

Published by AuthorHouse 04/15/2021

MAKING A JEWEL

CARVER LITERARY ARTS SOCIETY POETRIES,
SHORT STORIES AND ESSAYS

Dedication

Dedicated to Prudence Curry, the first African American director of the Carver Library that was held in the Carver Cultural Center. In 1905 The Carver Community Center began as the Colored Community House built on land bought by the branch of the NAACP. By 1930, it became the Colored Library Auditorium eight years later, as a tribute to agricultural chemist George Washington Carver and in the community, it became the hub for celebrations that included Masonic Lodge meetings, debutante balls and graduations. For over 75 years, The Carver Community Center has been the scene for many cultural settings. The names of the great legends like Duke Ellington and Ella Fitzgerald performed at the Carver Library Auditorium. The library will celebrate 90 years of service to the community of San Antonio, Texas from 1930-2020. The Carver Library is considered the Jewel on the east side of San Antonio. The community is grateful for all the hard work and dedication Mrs. Pruitt and many others have done for the city of San Antonio.

The Carver Library allows one to explore many lands without leaving the room or city. There are African American décor, computers, a learning center, children's library, a teen room and tons of learning activities for the young and the mature.

Antoinette V. Franklin has taught writing classes at the Carver Library since 2008 and established The Carver Literary Arts Society. The Carver Literary Arts Society writes and expresses new ideas and experiences. The following anthologies have been published: The Carver Literary Arts Society Anthology 2010, Set Your Compass to the Stars, and Imagination 2018 provides examples of capturing the spirit. Writing is the new adventure and reading is the new experiment.

The writers of the Carver Literary Arts Society are encouraged to read, write, and read and write again. "Learn something new every day." Always remember your culture and learn something about other cultures." Use your talent and do not allow others to exploit you. As a young writer, I have been told by teachers that I could not write, and that creative writing is different from academic writing. Creative writing frees the soul and expresses the mind's eye and imagination. Academic writing is boring and has its place to an area of academia and is regimented, but it is required for certain areas of education. This is concerned with extensive research, documentation, but it is still writing. As a writer perfect your craft by attending writing workshops, join a writing group. Write, look up new words, gather information and have happy writing moments. Reading is an experiment. Writing is the new adventure.

First African American Director of the
Carver Library

Forward

The African American community has always appreciated great storytelling. It is part of our DNA. Ancestors gathered in cabins and around fires and spun tales that delighted, thrilled and generally held us rapt. More recently, as we traveled back to family homesteads to attend family reunions, we heard tales passed down still.

That is why it warms my heart to write the foreword for this next anthology of stories and poems from the writers in the Carver Literary Arts Society (CLAS). Just as with previous collections of writing, this edition offers something special. It comes with tributes to the late John Lewis and George Floyd. One entry recounts a lesson in what it means to cast a vote; and another explores why education is so valuable to us. This collection is also special because it pays tribute to the late Prudence Lewis Curry, who served as director of Carver Branch Library, in San Antonio, Texas, from 1929 to 1958. May we always remember her example of hard work and determination; her love of her community and her ethic of growth through reading.

Finally, this anthology is a celebration of our culture, of who we are as a people and what we hold dear. So now sit back and enjoy these poems and stories. Then go tell somebody.

DL Grant

Acknowledgement

First, I give thanks to God for talent and blessings. Thanks to my sister Grace Banks for encouragement and providing stories. Thank you, Alexis, my sweet daughter, for giving me encouragement and laughter, Thanks to my dear cousin C. E. Lara for her editing skills and advice. I thank the Carver Literary Arts Society, D. L. Grant Carver Library Manager and staff. This has been a great experience.

Table of Contents

Poetry

Short Stories

Essay

Poetry

How I Got Over

How I got over

The song how I got over
Was sung by Mahalia Jackson
"How I got.
How I got over
You know my soul looks back
And wonder
How I got over…"
Our ancestors were strong determined people they lived through slavery, there wasn't an ignorant
African stolen on board those ships, the fact that knew they would never see
their homeland again, faced racial discrimination, segregation,
World War I and World War II.
Indignity, injustice, lynching, brutality.
God gave them strength of character to believe, hope and to survive,
to never give up, never give in, and nor give out.
To keep striving for the top of the mountain and reach the goal, "the eye on the prize."
They used African ingenuity passed from one generation to the next. after a
long journey, their offsprings are making the world better, reaching the
Summit.
"How I got over" was more than a dream, but the reality of the people who came before us.

(Permission granted copyright 1951. Originally written by Clara Ward)
How I Got Over hymn composed and published in 1951 by Clara Ward (1924-1972)

Antoinette V. Franklin

Why Vote

Many people were denied
Their right to vote
Women, Blacks, Hispanics,
Spanish speaking people,
People of color,
Native American/Indigenous people we're not considered citizens.
From the civil rights movement of
Dr. Martin Luther King
The Native American/Indigenous
People were granted citizenship.
My grandparents, and parents
Were segregated and had to pay poll tax to vote.
My generation was
Integrated, experienced the changes of the world.
"Say it loud
I'm Black and Proud.
I voted at the age of 18.
I was so excited and felt part of the situation.
How great to be an adult.
Be sure to investigate
Your choices and read about their background and voting ability of the persons selected.
Encourage those 18 years
Of age.
To register and
VOTE.
This is an important time,
I am excited and have mailed my ballot, you are important.
VOTE.

Tribute to Our Veterans

Valor of a warrior
Everlasting loyalty
Truth and justice
Encouraging others
Righteous service
A fighter for peace, freedom
Noble soldiers
Happy Veterans Day
Thank-you for your service.
We support you.

Antoinette V. Franklin

My father

Nathaniel Thompson Franklin born in 1921
Was a veteran of WWII.
He faced the segregation and hostility of racism, but said he would fight for freedom at any cost.
When he returned to the United States
He was treated very unfairly, treated less than a second-class citizen, but he believed in freedom.
He loved the United States
And brought his family
Up to be good citizens,
When there was a
Five-day war in the 70's in Egypt,
He told my mother and I that
He was going to reenlist.
My father was 50,
But he came home from work late and declared he had spoken to a recruiter,
Although the Army didn't call him and
The insurrection ended peacefully,
He said he was ready. and had made a stand because of the love of country and freedom.

Spring
Is a time for love,
For joy, for renewal. a time of beauty
And happiness.
When birds sing
And bees are buzzing
Joyfully,
Every tree and flower
Is in bloom.
I wish you peace and
Happiness
As we approach this spring

Beatrice Anderson

A wonderful thought

April poetry month 3 rd prize winner 2020
Be grateful
For good health let our senses enjoy
The awesome
Fragrance of flowers
Blooming in spring,
The freshness of
The air after a great
Down-pouring
Of heaven's rain.
Take time to smell
The roses.
Have a blessed day.

Beatrice Anderson

"This is My Shack"

This is my shack!
What is it to you?
For this I worked hard.
I came in at the end of the day thinking there were oppositions and trails too!
This sanctuary is mine, not for you.
It's my house;
This is my shack!
It's my house;
This is my shack!
I am blessed going, blessed coming back,
Tho' this dwelling be ever so humble,
I'm grateful to be able to say, this space is mine.
This is my shack.

Antoinette Franklin

Tom Howie's Artwork

Tribute to John Lewis

The year 2020 has been a very interesting, eye opening and thought-provoking year with the coronavirus, many sick people, dying people, and racism. People marching peacefully for justice.

John Lewis was one of the workers of the civil rights movement. Dr. King called him "The boy for Troy, "Congressman Lewis left marching orders for writers and activists to follow. He left a memory of hard work and enduring physical violence while caring for people. The most impressive thing about him was that he followed Dr. King's Nonviolence method of seeking justice. He forgave the man who had injured him during "The Bloody Sunday," march over the Edmund Pettus Bridge in Alabama. I remember seeing the horror of Bloody Sunday.

These words are a section of a piece he sent to the New York Times before he died. He left marching orders for writers, activists, people of color, and interested persons for change and justice. His last words were… Make sure they Vote. "We shall overcome some day…"

…Do net despair, do not become bitter or hostile,
Be hopeful, be optimistic,
Never ever be afraid to make noise and getting into good trouble
Necessary trouble will find a way out.
We are one people, we are one.
Congressman John Lewis
"The Truth about the Moral Universe is long, but it bends toward justice."
Dr. Martin Luther King Jr.

Vote
Vote
Vote

Antoinette V. Franklin

Tribute to Chadwick Boseman
November 29, 1976 –August 28, 2020
A young legend has left us too soon,
He was an actor with spirit and depth of
Energy, knowledge and presence and dignity.
He passed on the same day Dr. King marched on
Washington D. C.
A historic, justice minded man,
He was an "Old Soul" acting as
Jackie Robinson
James Brown
Thurgood Marshall
Black Panther
Chadwick showed
The depth of person and of being true to Blackness he was committed to justice to
be young gifted and Black and inspired kindness and pride for young people,
Rest in power our King.
Press on with pride forever.

Watching the movie Black Panther inspired me to write this tribute. We must watch out for one another and join. The world is angry, hurt, and filled with pain.

We must join as one. There wasn't an ignorant African stolen from the motherland. We are beautiful, talented, dearly loved and highly favored. We are made in the image and likeness of God. We are one. We, the people, are one.

Antoinette V. Franklin

Tribute to Breanna Taylor

She was 26 years old Match 13, 2020,
She was a precious angel was taken too soon,
She was a daughter, a friend, and a professional
With a promise for a better way of life.
She was asleep in her home and didn't know what was happening.
The NO KNOCK situation took her life
Leaving her mother in continued pain.
God bless her and others in this type of pain.
It is insane
A shame,
No justice.
Now the police will not
See justice for their action.
Do lives matter if you are
Black,
Brown,
Indigenous,
Women,
Poor,
It is not right
No justice,
Something must be done,
No justice,
The police need to be restructured.
Stop killing innocent people.
We keep Breanna Taylor in our thoughts and prayers.
Rest in Power.

Antoinette V. Franklin

Tribute to Justice Ruth Bader Ginsberg
March 15, 1933- September 18, 2020

2020 has been an unsettling year.
I was very sad to hear of her death.
She was a warrior woman
And fought for justice for everyone.
A great woman, she stood her ground.
We can learn from her example continue the fight for justice,
The right to be…
I am very discouraged with 45,
She stood her ground until the end.
But his day is coming.
She gave us the
Reasons to stand tall and fight for what is right.
I admire strong women
And honor her presence.
Thank you for all you have done
You are the gracious one
Thank you and
Rest in power.

Tom Howie's Artwork

Haywood Bethel

"A Life of Humor"

Many of you who read my first book
"Hayward's Humor," said that it was great.
Others have said they were very impressed, even though this one has been a long wait.
Many of you who purchased it because it made a perfect gift.
Some folk even said, "that it was filled with humor and gave them a spiritual lift."
Bringing you up to speed my book signing tours took me to many unbelievable places,
where I met and made new friends and left a million and one smiling faces.
It was very educational meeting people of all kinds and different walks of life.
And hear other talented storytellers and poets that stopped by to visit or so eloquently recite.
From Austin I traveled back home to South
Bend and Sandusky and see old friends, to entertain in support of worthy
causes and travel to other places that I had never been.
To Panama, Cancun, St. Thomas Virgin Island, Panama,
Paducah, Cape Girardeau, and Colorado Springs.
At each place I visited and met more people, who were doing some exciting things.
In my present state of mind, it appears very clear to me, that there are
still a lot of other places in my lifetime I would like to see.
My schedule at times has gotten a little hectic, but I'm bound and determined to reach my goal
of seeing as many other places as I possibly can before I am unable to travel or get too old.

Printed with permission Haywood's Humor Haywood Bethel Author

The Attacking Roster

It was early one Friday morning
I was about 8 years old, it happened about just like that
I never ever saw anything like this coming
It was the day that the vicious rooster attacked.
I had moved from the city to the country, just throwing rocks at birds,
dogs, and cats, but I never thought I would see the day
I would be subject to a vicious rooster attack.
Why I was just learning to shoot my 22 rifle, and hunting squirrels, rabbits and things like
that, before I realized I had entered his territory and be under his vicious attack.
He was justa strutin through that barnyard, scoping out the hens like he
owned the entire pack, until he saw me coming through the area,
That's when he decided to attack.
I threw down my rifle and started running, trying to get away from that crazy bird,
I was justa screaming and shouting, but my cries for help were never heard.
Now he had me pinned up against the fence, all I could see was his spurs and break beak in
my face, the only thing that crossed my mind, was, "I gotta get the hell out of this place."
Now my body was tired from flailing my arms and legs and he'd figured he'd won, so he decided to
let me go, with tears in my eyes, I ran back, picked up my 22 rifle so I could shoot that so and so.
I loaded it and took careful aim at him
As he strutted around with his head held high
I squeezed that trigger gently said to myself goodbye "Mr. Rooster," goodbye.
When all the big commotion was over,
I was made to pick and clean that ugly bird.
My grandmother prepared him for Sunday dinner
At the dinner table I never said a word.
Yes the preacher had come over for dinner and in between bites he finally
asked me why it was hard for me to chew on this tough bird,
I just felt like I wanted to die.

Many of you might not believe the story, but believe you me this tale of woe is true.
How would you feel if you were forced to eat a mean old rooster who had attacked you?
It took a long time for me to eat chicken, after many years I had refused
to give it a try for whenever I smelled it cooking on the stove
I couldn't stand to hear it sizzle or watch it fry.
Of course, the moral of this incredible story, is whenever you're under attack by a rooster
or anything else you fear in life you gotta remember "To always fight back."

Printed with permission Haywood's Humor Haywood Bethel Author

George Bussey

When you see
Yourself through
The eyes, mind
And hearts of
Those you love
And love you. It
Looks like you.

George Bussey

I looked in the mirror
And wondered if the old man I saw had anything to do with young man
I felt inside.

Connie Coleman

Celebrating June 19, 2020

Today on the day of June 19th, my heart was at rest.
Black Americans
In the state of Texas
Were set free
From slavery.
Two years after
The Emancipation Proclamation
Issued by President Abraham Lincoln
On September 22, 1862,
Slavery had ended for Black People,
Who were being ignored
By the United States.
The institution of slavery was destroyed by a government that betrayed
African Americans for white privilege, while slavery was acceptable.
June 19th should be a national holiday for All Americas to celebrate together.

Connie Coleman

Love in my Heart

There is love in my heart for my friend, who has hurt me in the past.
God spoke to me
When I was preparing for bed.
The moment gave me
Hope,
My spirit said
Love and forgiveness.
God will you
Overcome
Your situation,
Just trust him.

Connie Coleman

On a dark and stormy night

The winds were blowing at a high speed.
The midnight sky appeared pitch black.
The wooden house
Started to jiggle,
My nerves were at a dead stop when suddenly the windows in the living room began breaking,
I heard someone
Screeching,
Bobby, my dog began barking the rain began falling steady on the rooftop.
I ran
Ran upstairs
To my
Red, black and green
Bedroom.
My cell phone rang loudly,
While the weather
Outside raged,
I closed my eyes, tried to go to sleep.
The fear was real, on a dark and stormy night.

Tom Howie's Artwork

Sandra Ania Fergins

Lights, Camera, Action
April poetry month 2 nd prize winner 2020
Lights, Camera, Action
Lights
The world is in a turmoil
People in panic
Gripped with fear
Far and more
Camera
God is here
He sees your need through
His ever-watching eye
Focusing on the picture
Below
Action
He sends His love from above
Telling us always keep still, keep still
I am here for you, I am here
For you
Be patient……wait

Tom Howie's Artwork

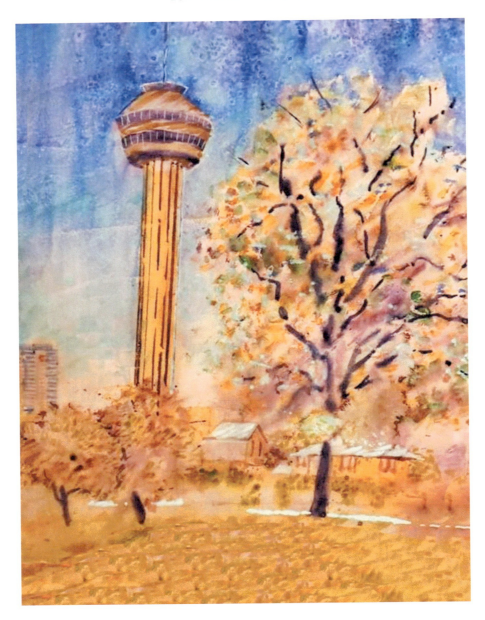

Sandra Ania Fergins

Negativity

Negative spirit drags you down
Leaves you with an endless frown
Bad thoughts, bad vibes spew endlessly
Throughout your day
Pray fast so that feeling will not last
A brighter day awaits when that negative feeling out…
You Cast

Sandra Ania Fergins

Keep your faith in the storm

Keep your faith in the plague
No matter what is thrown your way, stand up
For what you believe
The devil will attack you to matter which
Way you turn. Remember God is able to help
You withstand and will tend His guiding
Hand.
He is there for us and will never let us down.
Trust Him. Believe His word.
Stay strong through the storm.
Don't believe every lie the media throws your
Way. Their lies are meant to weaken your
Faith, come, what may.
Dear Christian, read the word. Pray fervently.
Lean on Christ and learn some more. He
Said I will never leave you nor forsake you
Cling to those loving words.
Keep your faith in the plague.

Sandra Ania Fergins

Come and Gone

Another life has come and gone
At the hand of a police officer
That same old song
Another black person perceived to do wrong
So sad to hear of your loss
For all to witness such a dreadful cost
Through tears and heaviness, we go through
Our day
Searching for answers and the right thing to
Say
Hold your head up high look to the sky
One day to our wonderful maker
We will fly…by and by…

Tom Howie's Artwork

Lou Hopson

The Lord Knows My Name

He knows my name
It is written in the palm of His hand
(His Tattoo)
He knows every hair on our heads.
Mighty and loving Abba Father knows our name and it is forever and forever calling…Amen

Lou Hopson

Bless You

I love you let me tell you my name
What will this morning be for me thank you for reminding me; he knows my name
Jesus loves me
Jesus died for me,
He died for me!
He knows my name!
Hallelujah!
Walk in His Presence
Blessings.

Lou Hopson

Acknowledgement to Fathers:
Happy Father's Day to all
Fathers, you are appreciated,
Honored and acknowledged
All fathers not just biological
Fathers, all fathers are
Acknowledged for their good work! To all who stepped up to the role of father for
the fatherless children due to death and other circumstances; thank you!
Also, to those who stepped
Up for absentee fathers because of illness or whatever reason,
You stood with concern effort to
Emulate Heavenly Father in His display of
Agape Love for all of us! God sees your work and He knows your heart.
As for me and the world, we see the fruit of your labor. It is not gone unnoticed
your good work was not in vain! Thank you for your good deeds as you continue
to pour into the growth and development. of future generations.
We would pause today to
Celebrate you and acknowledge you
On behalf of all little and big children,
Thank you!
Yes, thank you for not quitting, not
Giving up even when the mountain was
Rough and times got rough. You kept
Pushing as a woman traveling in labor.
You kept pushing
With great expectations for
The splendor, delightful and glorious of
The upcoming BIRTH of EXCELLANCE in
Our future generation; thank you!
For you, quitting was not an option. Therefore,

I honor you for the
Mentoring, raising and coaching our
Next generation.
I salute you and yelled out from the
Highest mountain in my heart, with honor, acknowledgement and love!
HAPPY FATHER'S DAY

Don Mathis

RUBY BERNADINE WALKER MATHIS GILLESPIE
A MOTHER'S DAY TRIBUTE
Her Story - April poetry 1 st prize winner 2020

Roared to life in the 20's

For a daughter of a square-dance calling man, crippled hip took you a while to walk, to stand.

Tempered in the 30's-

By the economy of that era.
What made others weak strengthened you.

Forged in the 40s –

The home front, the war,
Showed you could do a little more.

Conformed in the 50s –

Birthing babies and raising kids.
What you had to do, with what You had, you did

Tested by the 60s –

Revolution in the nation, the streets the home;
You held your beliefs. You stood Your own.

Resettled in the 70s

Making a Jewel

31

Seeds all sown, kids are grown.
You and our father finally alone
Expanded in the 80s –

You find more fulfilling work
And grow in the Lord and friendships at church
Entered new roles in the 90s –

Retired, and widowed, and joys of grand-parenting.
And then, near decade's end, married again.
Now the decade of the new millennium –

Do you know where your life will lead?
Whatever? It will be interesting, I believe.

20s-Bernadine was born Jan 34, 1925. She didn't work until age two due to a birth defect.

30s- Like many in the Great Depression, she learned to turn adversity to inventiveness.

40s- The support of civilians in WWII contributed to the global struggle for peace.

50s- The Baby Boom generation was part of this era. Mom contributed her part.

60s- Rebellious youth pushed the limits for many. Mom included

70s- Empty Nest? Not Mom and Dad! They vacationed around the country and Europe.

80s- No sooner had she retired; Dad died. But Mom found joy with new grandchildren.

2000s- The new bride moved hundreds of miles from family and friends-and thrived!

2010- Bernadine moved to her heavenly home on Feb 18, 2010.

Antoinette V. Franklin

Wisdom Words
Our priest Father Tom
Said God protects us
We are in the palm of
His hand and when trouble surrounds us
He closes His fingers
Around us.
Keep your faith.
Believe.

Father Thomas Fitzgerald
Heard during Mass celebration. St. Joseph has been my place
of peace and Father Tom helped everyone

Sulema Mendoza

No Justice No Peace
The poem was written during after the death of George Floyd 2020
He was handcuffed and the policeman kneeled on his neck

No Justice No Peace
No justice
No peace
When will the hate be released when will ignorance be decreased when
will the peace increase when will the cold blood freeze
Who will stand tall? and take action
Who will change?
What has happened?
Who will
Show heart &
Compassion
Who will step up is
All I'm asking
Where will our people
Find
Freedom
Where are the
Leaders when you need them where does it end give us a reason
Where is our
Guiding light
Our beacon
What direction are
We heading to
What intention are
We heading to
What intention are

We leading to
What is real
When everything is unreal
When everything is untrue
What is right if
We don't fight for you
Why are we accepting
Ignorance
Why others see indifference
Why are we losing our
Innocence
Why do they
Resort to
Pain and violence

Andrea Sanderson San Antonio's first African American Poet Laureate 2020

Precious Jewel

I want to borrow word from *Psalms and Proverbs* to describe how
love becomes sacred when unearthed from rock.
Through lineage, through blood thicker than the water and clay that make up my skin and sinew.
But the parts of us that will eternally continue are invisible and indestructible, not fragile, as our flesh.
So, I will press this precious jewel to my chest and move forward.
This may sound like sorrow, but there us hope wrapped in this lament.
For the years that I've spent picking up your mannerisms like smooth stones.
I've gathered your stories into this bosom.
They have ripened me to my bones.
I have grown up loving this nurturing matriarch from the start to the finish.
May your value increase, though your body diminished.
The sound of your laughter left my spirit replenished.
So, I will press this precious Jewel to my chest and move forward.
I have learned what it means to be concerned, from the way you weave
an inquisitive rhapsody into the composition of your words.
How your glittering eyes would telescope my constellations searching for obedience and honesty.
"Everything is fine, Granny" became my automatic reply.
How you would sigh from my lack of understanding, your
sensibility and sensitivity demanding I take heed.
Your thoughtfulness is expressed in word and in deed.
For a woman who spent her lifetime working until her body would no longer allowed.
For a woman who loved her children strong and proud.
For a woman who taught me to be a lady and let nothing go to waste.
For a woman that could create comfort in any space.
For a woman that would cook you southern soul with flavor and spice.
For a woman that would fuss over you to make every wrong turn right.
For without this woman I would not know life.
You are a radiant jewel that I will forever hold to the light.
I will press your precious memory to my chest and move forward.

Making a Jewel

Short Stories

A Day in Time

Beatrice Anderson

Tribute to Mothers

God established your role in life in Genesis: 2:28 "be fruitful and multiply; fill the earth and subdue it...:"

I salute you mothers for being able to wear many hats as you go about your daily tasks. You become a doctor, a lawyer, housekeeper, cook, banker, a free taxi, and whatever else is needed. Truly you must process the fruits the spirits, which are love, peace, long suffering, kindness, goodness, and self-control. (Galatians 5:22-23.)

We appreciate and honor you for these reasons: You make every moment in our lives a marvelous and memorable time. Observe close around you, seeing what is needed for their being. Tolerating all the things you do good and some not so good, you endure them. You take the time to teach your children about God's will for them.

Home is where the heart is, you strive to make it a happy and comfortable place.

Enthusiasm is shown in your spirit. You are interested in your children's lives and they are excited to be around you! Redeemed, yes, you are redeemed of the Savior. Christ is reflected in your daily walk as you relate to your children and others.

In conclusion, Mothers, you are a gift from God. According to Corinthians 13:13, we encourage you to keep the faith, hope, hope, and love, love most of all.

**Happy Mother's Day
Everyday!!!**

Beatrice Anderson

Family Tree

Trees, trees, Oh! So many trees just think there are so many trees. There are big trees, little trees, and even ugly trees. Wait, there are more trees, tall trees, short trees, slender trees, even fat trees.

A seed is planted in the ground. As time goes by it grows and sprouts into a young sapling. As time goes by it becomes a mature fruit bearing tree. Don't forget about the family trees, like those of humans, there are a kind of family too.

Usually, we think there's only good families, or bad families, as we think of the fruit as a good or worthless tree. But you must face facts that each good tree could have some defective traits and some defective trees could have positive traits.

Look at any tree, you'll find that good growth begins with a strong root system. strong roots get nourishment from good rich soil, plus the right amount of water, good air and sunlight. This results in this production of good fruit.

When looking at trees and onward the sky, comparing them to a human family; whether it be short, tall, big, or small. You'll see the strong trunks reaching upward toward the sky, spreading its mighty limbs upward and outward too, from the bigger branches and twigs. From the twigs comes the many clusters of leaves. What spring fort are the seed-bearing buds.

Time continues to move forward in due season and these become the first fruits of the tree. After the fruit is harvested and eaten, the seeds are planted for future reproduction, or it may be tossed into the trash and lossed forever.

Deep family roots extend to patents, and grandparents, great-grandparents, great-great-grandparents and further back in time. Think about the branches in the many families they represent, even the many leaves, like many children of many families. These children are seed bearing fruit of the future. These children are like the harvest of a tree being sent out in various destinations to be used for many purposes. This should be given joy and satisfaction.

The tree and man are both from a good tree or family which both have a strong root system. What is man, that thou art mindful of him thou son of man? And thou son of man, that thou visited him? For thou have made him a little lower than the angels and crowned him with glory and honor. Thou made him to have dominion over the works of thou hands; thou hast put all things under his feet. (Psalm 4-6, KJV). To God be the glory for the work of his hands forever.

Connie Coleman

Today is a good Day September 1, 2020

Something strange is going on. I say a little prayer for you. On this good day something strange is going on in the neighborhood. My neighbors are standing outside near the tall apple tree. No one is talking, the children are riding their bikes singing "Mary Mack, dress in black," suddenly I glanced at six police cars in front of the CVS. My hair had not been combed, the sister standing next to me was listening to Wendell B's song confusion, her hair was straight and purple. We locked eyes. She was wearing a Black Lives tee shirt. I heard someone say, hey! "Why are these people standing around?"

It was boiling hot my weave was sweating and the employee at CVS came outside waving a gun in her hand. The police officer knocked her to the ground. She started yelling "Make America Great." The two white women began chattering, "Our country is going insane."

Something strange is going. Granny, as she was affectionately called leaned into the window as the young man, stated they have made a mistake. She told her grandson I say a little prayer for you.

The Victory Garden

My god-sister Barbara McDaniel, Stevens, Granger told stories about growing up in the Wheatley Courts. This area provided housing for many families in San Antonio, including the lived in these facilities.

Barbara said what was used as a baseball field became the victory garden. The families bought seeds and planted gardens for the community. There were fresh greens, string beans, herbs, like sage. thyme, and other spices and vegetables. Mrs. McDaniel planted sweet potatoes in the shape of a V for victory. The blooms were very beautiful when in full bloom and gave hope along with substance to residents.

There was a grocery store, called Hysaw. My cousin Margaret Williams always talked about the kindness of the Hysaw family. When people didn't have money, Mr. Hysaw set up an account and provided items needed by the families. The people paid at the end of the week or the end of the month. There was a man who had chickens and a cow on land not far away. People could get fresh eggs, milk and buy meat and other items from the Hysaw grocery store. Several of the men had dug gardens where the baseball field had been. The men had dug up the field for their wives and their families for gardens.

There was a barber shop set up by Mr. Dibble where many men were able to get their license and worked as barbers. Mrs. Hicks had a beauty shop set up and many of the students attended Phyllis Wheatly were taught beauty care methods. There was a wood shop area for students as well. We have gotten rid of the things that helped families. The children no longer write in Cursive and technology has weakened the abilities of people.

The victory garden was a great idea and there is now another community garden that has been developed for families in the eastside community. Many of the older neighborhoods are trying to assist families in these areas for growth. There is a time to grow and give back to the community.

Thank-you Mrs. McDaniel, The Hysaw and Dibble families for their insight and the many others who made the east side a great community. The east side was very productive and had several black businesses. There were three taxi companies that were Black owned and operated. These companies were the following: Bellinger, Montgomery and Hartfield that provided taxi transportation, there were a black cleaner, black newspapers; The Snap Newspaper and The Register, The Life Saver Grill was a noteworthy restaurant and Mr. Dykes owned the Chocolate Bar on Commerce Street. The Sutton family was very involved in the community. Mr. Aycock had a Pharmacy on Pine Street, where young people could get an ice cream soda. There was Collins Funeral, Lewis Funeral, and Sutton and Sutton Funeral home. There was a funeral home on the west side and cleaners as well. But the biggest hub of business was on the east side. There was a black woman who owned a motel on Cherry Street, she was a friend of my grandmother. She told stories about the singers, and dancers who stayed at her motel because they were not welcome in the white establishments. I don't remember her name, but she always had a beautiful smile and talked about the people who came and stayed at her motel.

Stories told by Barbara McDaniel, Stevens, Granger

Liberty Hill

My family, the Crayton's, began in Liberty Hill, Texas and Rockdale, Texas. My great-grandmother Lizzie Crayton Dykes Vance was the midwife and country doctor. She always carried her black bag and took care of many illnesses. Her family, the Crayton's, had a lot of land before leaving Liberty Hill; she had given a large sum of land to her sister. Granny said she wanted Aunt Mazzella to have the property, she said, she wanted her to have it because her sister had 12 children. After the property was signed and sealed, Grandpa James Dykes knocked over the lantern causing the house to be burned down. My grandmother Ellen took the train and headed to the city of San Antonio. She took a job as a maid and moved the family to San Antonio. Her brother later joined the family in San Antonio. Aunt Isabelle moved to Troll, Texas with Uncle Marshal. My sister, Grace told me this story of how we came to live in San Antonio.

She said my grandmother Ellen and great-grandmother Lizzie never used any form of credit but paid for their purchases from Mr. Ott's grocery store on Walters Street that was down the street from St. Phillips College. Many of the areas around the grocery store had yards full of chickens.

This was a community area for the lower east side that was fields of undeveloped property. The higher east side was beginning in Denver Hikes and the lower east side extended to the area close to Our Lady of Victory School and Nebraska, now Martin Luther King. During this time the city had trolley cars for public transportation.

My mother and sister walked from 103 Achilles Street to Holy Redeemer Catholic School and then later to Wheatley High where my mother attended, and later my sister walked to Holy Redeemer Catholic School and later to St. Peter Clover High School. The streets were not paved. During this time and when they arrived at school, they had to clean their shoes.

My grandmother lived at 1015 Hedges Street, just around the corner from my great grandmother. My great grandmother had an outside toilet and there were many houses that had small farms and there was a Chinese man that had a small store. If we went to the store, we had to watch out for Javelina Hog, he would chase us. I remember when the East Terrace Courts were built. These were homes for many families. I was born in 1954 and I attended Holy Redeemer Catholic School and was closed in 1968 starting integration.

Story told by Grace Ellen King Banks

Antoinette V. Franklin

The Calico Christmas

My grandmother always told wonderful stories of growing up in Liberty Hill, Texas. She said their first Christmas was quite an event. There was a large pine tree in the old Springfield church, that had been decorated with popcorn, calico fabric, and snow. Some of the branches were lit with candles and apples and oranges were on the other branches. The fragrance was heavenly. Several children were seated in the front row since this was their first Christmas.

The people were singing Christmas songs while Mrs. Jones played the piano. When the song finished out came a large man with white whiskers and a red suite from behind the tree. He stopped and rubbed his round belly and said Ho! Ho! In a very loud voice. My grandmother, uncle and aunt and the other children had never seen such a sight. The children became frightened and ran to the rear of the church. My grandmother said she was running the fastest because she had to get to" mama." Many of the children ran to their families as well because they were frightened. The children didn't know the fat Santa was the Reverend dressed in the red suit. He had a very loud voice when preaching but had frightened the children on this occasion.

Antoinette V. Franklin

Tom Six

This is the story about Tom Six. This wasn't his real name, but he always showed up just in time for supper. He had been in the war and walked with a limp. He would gather wood, milk the cows and help pick fruit from the trees when needed. He would help whenever needed.

Tom Six knew when the families were preparing to eat because when the fire was blazing up the chimney the food was being prepared, but when the smoke was slow and steady, he knew it was time to eat. He could almost smell the roasted chicken, the baked sweet potatoes, the fresh stew or the baked bread. He would sit on the hill overlooking the valley near the San Gable River. He would visit a different family daily and always was welcomed.

There were times when he would sleep in the barn and help with whatever chores needed to be done. But the children when they heard the knock on the wooden door. The children responding here comes Tom Six, as the food was being brought to the table. Their mother gave them a stern look, and she would open the door and welcome their guest. The family said grace and enjoyed the meal. There were times Tom Six would play his fiddle and the family sang songs. Tom Six had a happy look on his face. He shook hands with their father and thanked him for his hospitality. Tom Six then gathered the blankets, heading toward the barn filled with hay and he slept soundly. This story made me feel warm thinking of the kindness shown to a person who didn't have a place to stay. I thank my grandmother for these stories when life was simple.

Stories told by Ellen Dykes Perryman born 1900-1986

Antoinette V. Franklin

The Cotton Stalk Doll

My mother was born in 1921 during the stock-market fall. She said times were very tough and there wasn't any sugar and cornmeal. My great grandmother had a garden. My mother made a doll out of a corn stalk and her hair was the corn silk. She said she played with the doll and tried to take care of her because that was her friend. She didn't have much but she was well loved.

After the stock market crash there wasn't much work and times were very tough. My grandmother stayed at the place where she worked and would take the trolley on some weekends to see the family.

Story told by Ruth Ella Lara Franklin Born July 24, 1921 Death July 19, 2000.

Liberty Hill

My mother Ruth Ella Lara was born in 1921 In Liberty Hill, Texas. As we are the descendants of Crayton's lived and worked the land. There were many returns for home going back to Rockdale and Liberty Hill. My mother said that Uncle Marshall would drive the model T for the visit. She said when they arrived near Austin before Onion Creek at the crest of the hill, the classic car reached a point before entering the city. The car would stall out and the family would have to stop and rearrange the car and shift the items around and then push the car up the hill. They would then see the welcoming site of the state capital building. Nowadays you can't see the capital because of urban growth.

Antoinette V. Franklin

Family Reunions

Our family would go for family reunions in Kyle, Texas on the Blanco River at Uncle George and Aunt Bessie. She was Uncle Bud's sister. It was always a wonderful meeting and greeting of the families, the Crayton's, the Gipson's and the Allen's. After the property was sold. The Family Reunions were held in San Antonio, at Daddy Sherman and Mama Susie's at cousin Panucho's Panchvilla, then we would meet at Comanche Park. Many of our family members have since passed away, but the memories linger on.

The love of family and keeping family history is important for passing history to the younger members, remembering the cultural exchange is important to us as a people and families should keep records. My elder cousin Susie Emma Moultry, Samson, Piper was the last of the first cousins of the clan, and passed away in November 2019. She and Uncle Tommy were the historians of the family. I loved talking with the learning stories about the family and our beginning. She achieved the family history at UT Austin. I shared many letters with her and tried to visit often after my mother's death in 2000. Her letters were uplifting and encouraging, and she always said, "I love my people."

I was blessed for my grandmother, Ellen Dykes Perryman, was the storyteller and my dad Nathaniel Thompson Franklin told great stories. My great-grandmother Lizzie Crayton, Vance talked about her grandmother Lizzie and her mother Ellen were both slaves and Great, Great, Great John and great, great, great, great-grandpa Mac came into being. I learned who I am, where I come from and what was expected of me. Cousin Susie Emma told me I would take over when she was gone. She and Cousin/uncle Tommy Crayton were the storytellers. Cousin Susie told me that was my duty quite a while ago and I am picking up the pen to start writing and keeping records, asking questions, remembering. I have been told by teachers that I could not write. I am grateful my mother told me I was a good writer. I have told writers to never stop believing in yourself. I have had to overcome jealousy and unprofessional behavior of those in charge with degrees. I encourage students to try different forms of creative writing and never give up.

A friend told me that academic writing is boring, make sure you don't allow anyone to steal your joy. Black people have always been kept back and the new test is considered not fit but that is wrong of society. We are all special being born in the image and likeness of God. My family began in Liberty Hill, Texas, Flatonia, and Lulling, where my father's people began. I am happy to share information with those interested. We must remember that there wasn't an ignorant African bought from the Motherland. We are talented and beautiful, dearly loved and highly favored.

I am happy my mother told me before she died that I was a good mother and to continue to be a good mother and that I was a good writer and to keep being a good writer. Remember your roots, "learn something new every day. Preserve your history, talk to your elders and find out the essence of your beginnings. I am Texas born and Texas proud.

Antoinette V. Franklin

The Cuban Crisis

We are now experiencing the Global Pandemic 2019. Many lives have passed from this horrible virus. But in my sixty-six summers when I was in the third grade the United States experienced the Cuban crisis. There were missiles pointed at bases in the United States. My family lived close to Fort Sam Houston Army Base. It was quite frightening. My mother would kiss me when she took me to school and she told me to be brave, listen to the sisters, if anything happened, she would come get me as soon as possible. She would place the Brown Scapular of Mount Carmel around my neck protection. Whenever I felt afraid, I would touch the Scapular and felt better. I felt that the Blessed Mother was praying for me. I am proud to be Catholic and pray often.

We had many bomb drills; The nun would ring a bell and we would get under our desks with our chins on our knees. Our teacher leads us in the Our Father and five Hail Mary's. It wasn't until I became an adult, I found out about those missiles as an adult if something had happened, we could have all been destroyed. The crisis was finally lifted, but it was very frightening. The Sisters of the Holy family took great care of our school community at Holy Redeemer Catholic School. I was born in 1954 and these were difficult times. May have been about seven or eight years of age. It seems like yesterday.

My mother bought many cans of vegetables, dried milk and she and my father talked about what might happen and we prayed for safety and protection. She also had candles and the city was asked to keep the streets lights off since we were so close to the Army Base. My parents had worried looks on their faces. He and my mother had decided not to make any new purchases in case anything occurred then they would be able to handle whatever that may have come up. Mother still bought cans of vegetables, bath soap, toothpaste and candles.

One day she told me we were going to go shopping at Karokins furniture store downtown. She selected a beautiful black china cabinet, a beautiful table, with two loveseats chairs and a black end table. The salesperson made out the ticket and said the furniture would be delivered next week. I was surprised and waited until we were in the car because as a child you were to be seen and not heard. I finally asked her about what daddy had said. She replied, in a matter-of-fact manner, "Well we are going to be blown to pieces anyway, so I may get what I want. I thought Ok!"

The news interrupted a program with a great deal of excitement and stated that the missiles were being removed and the cruise was over. My mother only replied, "now I have to pay for this stuff." She looked disappointed but continued to move forward and had the beautiful furniture, with lots of canned vegetables and canned meat in case of an emergency.

Antoinette V. Franklin

Everyone Must Get Vaccinated

In the 1970's there was an epidemic with Diphtheria that had spread to the entire city. The people were in a state and my mother being a nurse gathered her family together and stated we were going to have to be vaccinated. There were long lines surrounding the auditorium. We had never had any type of problem like that since. Now in 2020 we are experiencing the Corona 19 virus. As of April 2020, 60,000 people have died. This has been very frightening with prayers and the hard work of nurses, doctors, and health professionals. We are moving forward.

During this time frame there has been a hoarding of toilet paper now the grocery store will limit the amount of meat that can be purchased. My mother was a woman and I am grateful she taught me to be fragile. I thank God for her. She's been gone for twenty years. I think of her daily and love her dearly.

My grandmother caught the flu during the 1918, 1919 flu epidemic and was very ill. She lived to be 86 years old. My mother died of breast cancer at the age of 79. At this writing I have lived 66 summers. Writing helps me get things straight and helps me document history. Sharing these history events keeps memories alive.

Antoinette V. Franklin

2020 CoronaVirus dedicated to the memory of the many people who lost their lives during this time.

This pandemic spread rapidly across the world. There were deaths, many cities were closed, for two months, the city of Los Angeles had clearer skies when there was smog and the San Antonio River was clear and you could see the bottom, toilet paper, hand sanitizer were hoarded, and meat was rationed. Sports activities were cancelled, along with the closure of schools, colleges and business. There was an empty feeling seeing the vacant buildings, playgrounds, and downtown areas.

Things are slowly becoming a new normal. People are wearing masks and gloves. There are many unsettling areas and situations, but people are taking a stand and moving forward one day at a time. We have had to shelter in place for two months and be in by 8:00. This experience has been very different, but I have thrown away unnecessary things and completed writing. We are awaiting a vaccine for the CoronaVirus. A change is gonna come.

People have done the shelter in place and are doing the safe distance, six feet, now some of the restrictions have been lifted. Some areas of restriction have now been extended. Many of the schools will host graduation ceremonies until June. This has become a new normal. I put on my mask and gloves before getting out of the car. I remember my great-grandmother, grandmother and mother putting on their hats and gloves to go out, now I wear gloves and a mask for protection. Times have changed, I guess the world has made the changes. One thing I know God is in control and I am grateful. God will make a way. My grandmother always said, "The sun will shine in your back door."

More bad news was announced about a dam that had broken in Michigan and 10,000 people were homeless. I was watching Tyler Perry's "Meet the Browns," the most touching part was when the mother was crying because of not having money and needing to pay the electricity. I remember waiting for my baby to go to sleep so I could cry, When I thought she was asleep I began to cry, when I heard this sweet voice saying, Mommy, "Why are you crying? I told her I was sad because I didn't have any money. She ran into her bedroom and returned with a handful of change and placed it into my hand. She said don't cry you got money. I cried even more. God had given me a blessing to see through the eyes of a child.

This time during the corona virus makes us reflect on the goodness of God. He has been so good to us all the time. We are still filled with health. God had been good because it could be worse. I am praying more for God's children, those experiencing the coronavirus, the people in Detroit, people filled with anger, destress, loneliness, and despair. I am grateful to know there is God. We must look to the hills from which cometh our help.

Another unfortunate incident happened over the weekend. A Black man was killed by a police officer. The whole country has been protesting and violence has touched the country. George Floyd was a security guard and seemed to be a peaceful God-fearing man. He was handcuffed and was on the ground. The police officer kneeled on the neck of George. The man cried out stating he could not breathe. He called for his mother, who had died two years before.

Someone had a video, all things went to street violence, burning, smashing windows, in many cities. Many people have died, and they are still seeking a cure. I feel this disease was started in a lab and we are paying the price.

Antoinette V. Franklin

The New Stove

My mother was a true queen with beauty, charm and grace. I am grateful for her presence and wisdom. My mother worked the 11:00 p.m. to 7:00 am graveyard shift as an LVN, scrub tech, in the operating room of our county hospital, while my father worked for the railroad. My parents had a partnership that worked out to where my mother took my brother and I to school and picked us after school, and my father was at home with us at night.

Since they had such strange working hours, breakfast was very important to our family, because we rarely had the opportunity to have breakfast together. One Saturday morning my father was home from work, and I awakened to the smell of bacon frying in the kitchen. When I inquired about the delicious smell, I found he had made pancakes also. He said, "He wanted to surprise my mother with breakfast," and asked for me to set the table.

My little brother sat glued in front of the TV watching cartoons while I busily placed the china, silverware and linen napkins for the occasion. I cut fresh pink roses from the rosebush outside. The dining room table reminded me of the table settings like the ones I had seen in my mom's *Southern Living Magazine*. I knew mama would be pleased. It was nearly eight fifteen and my mother would be arriving soon. My father and I went outside to wait for her arrival and greet her. It was a nice spring morning and we were serenaded with the song of the birds. My father remarked about cutting the grass and weeding in the garden later. Our green and white Ford Fairlane was being carefully driven by my mother nearing our driveway. I could see my mother's head bouncing to the sound of the music on the radio. When we thought she was going to signal and turn into the drive, she waved like a queen in a parade and turned at the corner passing the school. We watched as the brake lights disappeared around the corner and descended the hill. My father said, "What the…?" and dropped his jaw in confusion. I saw the look of concern on his face and tried to reassure him. I said, "Daddy she'll be back, she's listening to a song on the radio." I added, "She does this all the time." "She likes to finish the tune before turning off the engine."

My mother loved music, all types of music, country and western, Mexican Ballads, Benny Goodman, Count Basie, Duke Ellington, Fats Waller, Nat King Cole, Nina Simone, B.B. King and Bobby Bland anything with a good beat. She said the music helped her to stay awake, make it home and helped her stay happy when she felt sad. She and my father had a strong belief in God.

As she circled the block, she pulled into the driveway as if nothing had happened and said in her sweet little girl voice, "Well good morning." She smiled her radiant smile and kissed us both on the cheek. She was very surprised by breakfast and told me how pretty the table looked.

We had many special moments filled with happy times together. There was one occasion one late afternoon, after grocery shopping and returning from the laundry mat, my mother asked, "What we wanted for dinner?" My brother said chicken that was his favorite. I said, "I wanted to have breakfast." Mama replied, then breakfast it is. She made scrambled eggs, toast with strawberry jam and a big glass of milk. We sat in the dining room drinking from her special silver goblets. The goblets she had gotten with the Texas Gold stamps she had saved, and I had placed the stamps into the booklets. We had an elegant dinner setting, while wearing shorts and sandals sitting at our dining table. I got my first black doll with long pretty lashes and my brother got a Tonka Truck with the other books of stamps. There were S & H Stamps and Top Value Stamps. I don't remember what stores had stamps, but there was HEB, Handy Andy and Piggly Wiggly. I remember. I collected and placed them in the books and was ready to shop with my mother.

The table was always set for dining, a nice tablecloth and napkins and we often used the best stuff. Mama said, "We are to use the best for family and not to wait for company." She added that, "We were special." She always said, "We were the diamonds in her life."

On the day my mother purchased a new stove, we were supposed to be shopping for new work overalls for my father. She found a stove with a top range and broiler and fell in love with its elegant copper tone color. The stove had lots of storage in the bottom compartment. One of the burners had a timer set to simmer food and turn itself off in order not to overcook your special sauces. That's what the salesman said.

My mother said, "We'll take it," as she whipped her revolving charge card out, she added, "When can it be delivered?" My mother didn't have to consult with my father about purchases because she handled the finances for our family. The salesman looked surprised and added, Yes Ma'am.

My father usually didn't complain about her purchases, because he trusted her judgment. We later went to the men's work clothes department and paid cash for the overalls.

My mother was glowing when she told my father about our new stove, describing it in detail. She loved the copper-tone color and all the special features. The stove did everything except for season the food and placed it in the pot, that's what she told my father. The oven and broiler had a self-timing feature that turned itself off automatically and alerted you when the cooking was completed. My father said, "He would have a friend pick up our old stove."

The new copper-tone marvel was delivered bright and early on Monday, after all the adjustments were made the stove was ready for cooking. They manufacturer provided a new cookbook. The stove had a covering to hide the burners and would slide back for cooking. It was quite pretty, all bright and shiny sitting in our moderate kitchen. It took up quite a bit of space, more than the original white stove with four burners, with the broiler on the bottom.

Mother was too excited to cook. Monday, we had leftovers. Tuesday. we dined on hamburgers from Whopper Burger, around the corner. Wednesday was chicken from the colonel, Thursday was fish from a drive through restaurant, and Friday was tuna fish sandwiches without the boiled eggs. Saturday came with the brightness of spring and chores to be completed, after cutting the grass and trimming the yard. My father settled to watch the baseball game and my mother served the family spaghetti my grandmother had sent over.

My father had a funny sense of humor and he said, "I guess I'm going to have to get the old stove back from Jackson," as he slyly grinned at my mother. My mother asked, "What are you talking about?" He continued, "Well we haven't had a home cooked meal in a week." Mother laughed and said, "I didn't want to mess up my new stove." My father said grace and we began to eat our meal.

Daddy wasn't going to let her get the best of him and he responded, "I guess I'd better start buying my own work clothes because this is the most expensive pair of overalls I have ever had. My mother just gave him that look that stated she wasn't "studying him" as she refilled his plate with spaghetti.

We kept that stove for quite a time and often laughed about the overalls. My mother cooked often on the beautiful copper colored fancy stove.

Joanna Hargrave

Dragon Breath

Julie was finishing dressing for school. The sun was shining, and the birds were singing. Julie looked at her reflection in the mirror and smiled. She remembered what her dentist, Dr. Rowe said, you don't want to have dragon breath. He told her the story about dragon breath. Julie had asked him What is dragon breath? Dr. Rowe told her about the fire breathing dragon and how people would run away from him. He didn't have friends, no one wanted to talk with him. He told her that it was important to brush your teeth after every meal and to floss often, and to also rinse your mouth, that would help prevent dragon breath. After the dragon brushed his teeth every day, flossed after eating, and gargled his mouth, she no longer had dragon breath. Julie liked this story and she smiled. She didn't want to have dragon breath and she had a new toothbrush with mint flavored floss.

Frances Phillips Lee

My Black History Story

The American Bible Society stated, "That less than half of Haiti's population could read. "I grew up in South Bend, Indiana, the home of the Ku Klux Klan, a group known for the hatred of Blacks then and now. I was convinced all my teachers who taught in elementary school were members of this organization. I would like to share some information that came as I was Schomburg Center for Research in Black Culture arrived. The center is eighty-five years old. Arturo Alfonso Schomburg, as a boy was told by a teacher, that Black people had no history. She further implied, "You are nothing because you came from nothing." I hope she lived long enough to see the fine center he started. The above quote about Haiti reminds me of my love for reading, which was instilled in me by my mother. She read the Bible every day to herself and to her children. She found time to read the daily newspaper from cover to cover every day, even the obituary.

There were six children in my family, and we were poor. I was enrolled in kindergarten when I was six.

I came from a family where the children were seen and not heard. I didn't know I was supposed to talk, for a long time I didn't. Shortly after my arrival, I was sent to the nurse. It was determined that I needed glasses. I was teased and made fun of by the children all the time. They had never seen anyone with glasses, except for old people. I hadn't seen anyone either. This was a minor adjustment I would experience in the classroom. It was a very traumatic experience.

Because my parents were poor, they were unable to pay the dollar seventy-five cent book fee, and I was not given any supplies. The white children sat at a large table with pencils, paper, crayons, scissors and many piles of books. This made it easy to keep the lie going, that black children could not learn. While all the Black children sat in little straight chairs on the opposite side of the room. I spent most of my semesters in that location in many classrooms. Benjamin

Harrison School had a lovely library, but we couldn't look at the books. We were not allowed to take the books out of the room. There was a book closet in the room. When the door was opened to the closet, there were so many books they would spill out all over the floor. I asked the librarian once, if I could take two books out overnight and promised to return them the next morning. She said, "No, she was not allowed to give books away." One day the janitor finally came and dumped all the books into a large trash can; my eyes still filled with tears, even no. The South Bend Public Library also refused us entry. If your father didn't have a job, you were not issued a library card. The rationale was that if something happened to the book, there were no funds available to replace their book. A friend of mine Mildred Sanders both of her parents worked, and she had a library card. She would then check out two books, one for her and one for me. I would have to wait for her outside since I didn't have a card; I could enter. There was always someone sitting at the door checking if you had a card. We would meet again when the books were due.

The library had a large music room with many instruments. There were some I had never seen before. The rental fee for the instrument along with the lessons my parents could not afford, was another way of denying us access to the arts. Proving again the lie that Black children could not learn. When I entered the eighth grade, a teacher told my mother I could read and learn. She told my mother to take me out of school and find me a job. My mother threatened her (I cannot tell you what my mother said). Nothing changed, I think it got worse.

We were denied entrance to many public places such as: swimming pools, roller skating rinks, ice skating rinks, and bowling alleys. We were not allowed to sit at the counter at Woolworth's a 5 and 10 cents store. We had to take your food outside. There was one movie theatre that was open only on Saturday afternoon. It was dark, smelly, dirty, and we could only sit in the balcony section; one time was enough for me, so I never went back.

Finally, time passed, and I was off to High School, this experience changed my life. A counselor, who recognized my enthusiasm and excited me being there, took an interest in me and she guided me along the way. The first year I made the honor roll which convinced me of what I already knew that I could learn. When time came for graduation there was no money for college, or programs for scholarships. When the time came for me to leave high school I cried. The desire for reading, my love for books never left. I was able to buy a book whenever I wanted to. What a thrill!!! At one time, I had more books than I had clothes.

I later married and when my spouse walked away, I decided to go back to school. I graduated, made the Dean's List and received my degree. I was able to teach Kindergarten Classes at James Memorial Christian Academy for 12 years. Every child I ever had in my classroom left reading. Two of my former students Brittany Rideau and Michael Gates are both now enrolled at major universities and are doing quite well. My advice to everyone is, "Don't listen to the devil's lies." I was told I could not learn and was teased constantly about my glasses. Every day I was reminded that I am Black. Many adults laughed at me when I told them I was going back to school. They said, "For what??" You are the only one who knows what God has spoken to you.

He has told you what He wants you to do with your life. You are never too young or too old to learn. Making you Black was God's idea. It's never too late, just go do it!

C. E. Lara

Awakened [(c)] 7/15/2020

Earlier in the evening, my roommate, Yoli and I sat down to a delicious dinner. We enjoyed my homemade meatloaf, whipped mashed potatoes with gravy, and a zucchini casserole. I blew on my fingers and puffed out my chest. I was happy because the food had turned out like one of my idols, the late, great professional chef Edna Lewis. Over the years, I had memorized quite a few of her recipes and had perfected them. With these, I had added my own twist, making them seem like they were my own. It didn't matter how tired I was, my long-time tradition was to kick-off a long-weekend with comfort food, laughter and relaxation. Not great for the waistline but good for the soul. We cleaned our plates. Groaned and pushed back from the table.

Later on, the sweet smell of homemade buttermilk pound cake filled the kitchen. Yoli had dished-up the lip-smacking delight. And to top it off, strawberries with whipped cream. The cake was so light, it would melt in your mouth. My mouth watered as she cut into the golden-brown delight. Under protest I said "I'm still full. Just a small slice for me." Ignoring me she piled on the strawberries and whipped cream. "Oh, you're wicked, girl" I laughed. I took a bite and said

"hum, this cake is so light, it's melting in my mouth. Cut me another slice." She said, "girl, I'm cutting me a big slice from the git-go. I am not cheating myself," and cut herself a healthy slice of cake. We stuffed ourselves. Eyed each other from across the table, leaned back, and looked at our bulging stomachs. As good friends do, almost at the same time we exclaimed "Oh, that was good!" I laughed and said, "Yoli, girl, why did you let me eat so much?"

Groaning we vouched, "we're hitting the gym tomorrow. Pushing the chair back, slowly getting up, I started the usual routine, kitchen detail and storing leftovers. Ten minutes after nodding off and her head jerking awake. Yoli had a burst of energy. She joined me in cleaning. Yawning, stretching, she exclaimed, "Liz, girl, I am so glad I don't have to get up early in the morning. We haven't been off at the same time for months." She said, "I know one thing I'm doing. I am finally going to sleep in!" She finished clearing off the table.

After cleaning-up the kitchen we watched the evening news. There wasn't anything interesting happening. We had a marathon of yawning and stretching. Our heads rolling and nodding. We decided to call it a night. We headed off to our respective rooms on the opposite ends of the house.

Yoli called out "good-night girl". Smiling, she approached her quaint decorated room. She pulled off her blouse. Bra next, exhaled, whew. What a relief. Grabbed her pink silk gown. Struggled out of her pants. Threw everything in the hamper. It was as if her bed welcomed her with open wide arms. She fell into it hard. She snuggled onto the goose down pillows. Then remembered, "oh yeah, the darn CPAP machine." She sat up, struggled to fit the mask onto her face. And turned the machine on. The usual "humming sound" lullabied her into a deep sleep.

I called back, "See you in the morning girl." My room was several steps from the kitchen and near the front door. I slipped into my favorite comfy, black cotton jammies. Then glanced at the wall to check the security alarm. Yep, it's set. The red light is on. We're secure. Can't forget to pray. On my knees, thank you Jesus. I made it through another week. Now I am ready for some sweet dreams! Zzzzz … me and Denzel in Turks and Caicos. Yes, Idris, I'm available to go to Fiji. Ohh, Boris, Maui is …

Humm, I was sleeping "so good", breathing deeper, slower. I heard a sound … clank. My eyes fluttered. I heard the sound again. It was louder this time. I turned to look at the clock on my nightstand. It was 3:50 AM. I turned over to try to get back to my dream. Again, a succession of "clank …clack". I was gradually awakened out of my peaceful state by this annoying, persistent sound. I frowned and thought "why is Yoli leaving out of the front door? Didn't she say she was off from work today?" I turned over and gradually I recalled, "She parked back in the garage … didn't she?" Groggily, slowly I looked over at the clock again. This time the sound was more pronounced. I heard "thud … clunk … thud … clunk." I scrunched-up my nose and thought, "Now, lawd what is that noise?"

Slowly feeling more awake, my eyes started blinking slowly at first. Then faster. Faster still. I struggled, trying to focus on my surroundings. Slowly looking around. I asked myself, "where are my glasses?" Feeling around on the bed with my right hand. I realize, oh, yeah, here they are on the nightstand. My ears perked-up. Apparently now someone is at my door. With a key I thought? Is that a key being inserted in and out of the keyway, "clank …clank"?

Am I dreaming? I started shaking my head, blinking my eyes, trying to wake myself up.

Wow, I have got to focus. Then, I hear it again! Someone IS trying to break down - kick-in! MY! FRONT! DOOR ! **THUD!!** (*There is a pause*) … BAM**!!** (*There is another pause*). Now the sounds are more rapid! **THUD, THUD!! BAM, BAM!!** Were the sounds ringing in my ears!! OH – My GOD!! I sat up fast. I swung my legs out of bed! My feet were searching helplessly to find my slippers. I know they were left right there on the floor before I got into bed. I am telling myself, "Liz, get it together. Get your focus and composure. Heck no, there's no composure. I am scared!" (*I hear the sounds bang again*) **THUD. THUD!! BAM, BAM, BAM!!** The sounds are still invading my ears!

My eyes darted around my room. It is dark, except for a sliver of moonlight shining through my circle top window. My trembling hands grab my cell phone. I am looking for the SWANN security app. I had to check the camera to see what the 'hades' is going on. Who is at the front porch at this hour? OH MY GOD!! IT IS A MAN KICKING HARD AT MY FRONT DOOR. I hear mumbling "Freddie let me in. I know ya in thur man"; and some other inaudible sentences.

Well, my heart starts beating faster. My hands tremble and shake even more!

I called 911 … a female operator answered "911, what's your emergency?" My voice cracked as I said, "Hello". I cleared my throat and took a deep breath. Nervously I start speaking again softly to the 911 Operator. I inhaled slowly and said, "someone is trying to kick down my front door". I gave myself a quick pep talk *"girl control yourself - breathe slowly"*. I softly plead, "help me please." The 911 Operator in a nasal, but concerned voice says "Where's the emergency." In a low tone I started telling the 911 Operator the situation outside. And gave her my location.

I started quietly tip-toeing my way to the other side of the house. As I quickly passed the front door, I could hear this guy kicking and yelling "Freddie let me in." His yelling and kicking were echoing in my ears as I raced at breakneck speed toward Yoli's room. It seemed to take an eternity.

She, of course, was in a peaceful, deep sleep. CPAP machine humming; her mouth slightly open. She was lightly snoring! Thump-thump that was the sound of my heart beating so fast! I didn't want to scare her, so I tried to compose myself. I softly called out her name, "Yoli". No response. "Pssst!" I called a little louder "Yoli, Yolanda." Again, no response. Okay, now, I know she's not dead, she's snoring.

I could still hear this guy at the door. I checked my security app; he was still kicking and yelling. He hadn't lost any energy. Oh my gosh! He just stepped back and lifted his leg so high. Yikes, he planted his big foot on the door … BAM! I start praying "Jesus! Oh, GOD PLEASE don't let him kick in the door. PLE-E-E-ASE!!" I am scared and need some back-up. I GOT to wake her up. I believe the more the better, power in numbers! In other words, I need just some help!! This time, I turned on the light. I yelled at the top of my lungs. My voice rang out so loud, I almost scared myself. I hollered, "YO –LA –N—DA!!"

She shot straight up in bed, looked around like someone had jabbed her with a pin. I don't know what that 911 Operator must have thought. "What-a-at?" she sleepily asked. Looking around trying to get her bearings about her. She started roughly pulling at the CPAP mask trying to get it off her face. Rubbing her eyes. Throwing her head back. Opening her mouth wide, and yawning. She narrowed her eyes, squinted at me and asked "what's wrong?" My eyes were huge with fear. My voice was shaking, I murmured glancing toward the front door, "girl, a man is trying to break down the front door!" With a bit of a shriek she responded, "Huh? What you say?" She took a long, deep breath and swallowed so hard I could hear it. Her eyes got as big as saucers. Our eyes locked, a thousand and one adventures over the past twenty years must have flinted through each of our minds. We looked at each other and here we go. We have been 'ride or die' friends so I guess this situation qualifies, we were both SCARED!! We could hear him still kicking the front door and yelling "Freddie let me in!"

We started toward the front door, moving with a purpose. I had my back-up Yoli. The 911 Operator had called the police. I started thinking, "hum, where are they? In all fairness, it seemed like it had been a long time. I looked at the clock on my phone, it really had not been that long." We rushed down the hall. When we got to the living room we paused, hearing this dude. He hadn't lost any energy. He was still kicking. Still screaming, "Freddie, come on man! Let me in dammit!" "Open this door!"

Like the characters, Nakia and Okoye in *Black Panther*, we rushed toward the front door. Now, Yoli has a deep, sultry voice. She actually has a range of a couple of octaves, so it can go really deep. In fact, she has hoodwinked some folks on the phone a time or two. These folks actually thought they were conversing with a man. Yoli blurted out in the all-time deepest voice I have ever heard, "ain't no Freddie here, get away from here." Then I added my part. It came out like a high-pitch shrill "go on, get away from here." Clearing my throat, I thought to myself, "ok now Liz, where in the heck did that mess come from?" I'll admit, it was kinda shocking. I let the fierce duo down a bit. Well, let's just say I'm glad I had my 'ride or die' for back-up with me. We waited for a hot second, then sneaked a peak at him through the curtains.

The guy staggered down the steps, oops he almost fell. He thrust his hands in his pockets. He paused for a moment. Then, he turned around and looked back at the house three times. Picking-up his pace, he tottered down the sidewalk. Yoli and I looked at each other and whispered simultaneously "*what was he looking at?*"

We looked at each other in total amazement and mouthed "wow, did this just happen?" We gazed out to get a good look at him for a description to give the police. The 911 Operator, still on the phone asked "what's going on? The police are en route. Are you ladies okay?" I exhaled and said, "yes, we're okay. He just left, staggering going east down the street. I hope the officers can spot him."

Three police officers, Carter, Doyle, and Clayton from the local station arrived shortly afterward. They talked to us about the events, and huddled around my phone to review the playback on the security tape. They informed us that they had conducted surveillance in the neighborhood while they were en route.

Officer Carter, seemed to be in charge. She was tall and towered over us. But she had kind brown eyes with a calming smile and voice. She looked like she could have been a model if she hadn't wanted to serve on the police force. Tonight, I'm glad she chose to be a police officer.

After the cursory introductions, she said "now we will conduct a surveillance of the house.

Afterwards we'll sweep the neighborhood again."

Officer Doyle, a tall, lean guy was quite striking. Officer Clayton, ruggedly attractive, was shorter than Officer Doyle, but taller than Officer Carter. Officers Doyle and Clayton, walked around the house with their searchlights looking to see if the guy might be hiding, he wasn't.

Officer Carter stayed and took the report. Sometime later, Officer Doyle, rang the doorbell and reported nothing appeared to be disturbed. He assured us again that they would continue conducting a surveillance around the neighborhood.

For a couple of hours, Yoli and I would peek out the curtains. We saw police cars as they drove slowly down the street and by the house. We would see them shining their lights in neighbors' yards, looking for the guy.

I glanced at the clock. Wow, it was 7:55 AM. We were still sitting in the living room. We looked at each other; and talked about the unbelievable events that had just transpired. As good friends do, almost at the same time we declared, "no working out today!"

Weeks have passed. Months have passed. They still haven't found the guy. Where did he go?

There has not been any trouble since – thank God. My theory – there were angels surrounding and protecting us that night. I have tried to think about another explanation for the door not giving in – but I cannot. You see the front door is made out of oak and the top portion holds beveled glass. The police were amazed that the door did not give in. They commented on the assailants several footprints all over the door. Had he aimed his foot just a little higher, the glass could have been smashed. And, possibly a totally different ending to this story.

I know God's angels provided protection that morning when I was awakened.
"God will put his angels in charge of you to protect you wherever you go." Psalm 91:11 GNT

Essay

Why is Education Important?

My Favorite Library Stories

Making A Jewel
Why is Education so important?

Antoinette V. Franklin

My Father's Wisdom - I

My parents were strict about getting your homework, going to school and getting an education. They were very proud people. They worked hard and were black and proud before it was in fashion.

I was about eleven years old and had completed my chores, washing dishes, drying them, and putting them in the cabinet. I hadn't completed my homework problems, there were, about six more math fractions problems, math wasn't my favorite subject. I thought I could watch my favorite program; The Patty Duke Show and I would finish it later. I really liked the show. Patty was funny and dressed cute, I love skirts and sweaters. The show was about her cousin from England. I liked her British accent.

My mother was an LVN scrub nurse and worked the 11 to 7 shifts at Bexar County Hospital. My dad worked for the Missouri Railroad as a Carman. There were certain duties I had to get done before getting my mother up for work at 9:30. I would wake her up at 9:30 each night for work. I would make her instant cup of coffee before she went to work. We were to be inside the house before 6:00. She went to bed and was quiet while she was sleeping. We got our baths and did our homework. I looked after my brother and helped him with his homework. My father was home from working in Taylor and had a week off. He was usually out of town on his job.

Antoinette V. Franklin

My Father's Wisdom – II

My dad and brother were watching television when I asked my father if I could watch the show. There was about 15 more minutes before showtime. My father's answer to my request was: Have you finished your homework? I replied I had done all my chores and only had one more page to finish.

My dad was a philosopher and usually asked questions while teaching a lesson. He had a great sense of humor and would say things to make you think. The program was only thirty minutes and I couldn't see why It would matter. My father knew I didn't like math and I had struggled with the fractions. My father could figure in his head. I had to count on my fingers and toes and on someone else's to get the answer.

The lecture began honey tell daddy, do you have a job.? I replied no. I do work around the house and help mommy. Then he asked if I had any money? I replied yes, I had five dollars. I was saving to buy the new Sam Cooke Album "A Change Is Gonna Come". I had heard it on the radio and thought it was so pretty. My father wasn't finished and asked who took care of me, I replied to him and mommy. He then said my job was going to school and that was very important. And I was to help my mother. He added that the people on TV were making money and I needed an education. Since I didn't have a job or a lot of money. I was depending on him and my mother. I had to study and get an education.

I knew the program was out of the question when he added now baby, you will make daddy very happy if you finish your homework. He said bring it here and I'll help you. He did just that and reviewed it with me. He kissed my cheek and gave that mischievous and we worked the problems. He worked with me and told me I was catching on. I learned these methods to help my students understand like my dad took time with me. I learned to embrace a new way of understanding the subject.

I didn't see the show and finished my homework and worked with my dad. I often think of him and I thank him for his wisdom. I thank-you Nathaniel Franklin for love and wisdom. I still don't like math, but I taught GED Math, Science, Social Studies, reading and Writing for fourteen years. I found simple books to help me assist students in learning. I had to learn to help other students who were having difficulties. That is why education is so important. I have learned to never give up and always keep on trying.

Lou Hopson

Today a love one asked me:

Why can't our leaders live to a ripe old age like Mandela? Tutu?...

My response:

Please know the glass ceiling was not just for WOMEN. The reason is The Glass Ceiling is for

"The Black Man. Look around you; we have plenty of Rising Black Leadership. They do exceedingly well in their "lane." When they get into "The Main-stream" things start happening to them. For example: These lead to defame, shame, jail, or death, etc. They are stopped sometimes by their own people who don't have vision, sometimes they are stopped by themselves due to lack of self-control, or lack of focus, not "keeping their eye on the prize…"

Can you imagine what would have happened if Jesus was on the road to Calvary, if He had not been focused. Jesus saw the joy of what He's doing. He saw "me," Hallelujah!

The original plan was to bring the Blacks here and for us to stay in bondage. They did not know we would multiply. They did not know we would become educated. They did not know how much God loves us. They did not know the Lord taught us how to fight! So, their plan B started…

What they did not know is we are jealous of one another. What they did not know we would betray one another to get to the front, the (glass) top. They knew we would deny our family to be their "friend." They knew we would kill our own. They knew we would not teach the next generation. However, they taught their own children. What they did not know we would turn from "The True and living God" and start serving their gods (cars, houses, jealousy, sex, and other things we made idols.

They knew that we would talk at the wrong time and act by emotion, without logical or prudently thinking. They knew our actions would be based on fear, anger, "ignorance," and jealousy, destruction, etc. They know us and when they don't; cannot trust us we disappear! They knew we would be SILENT until we are not anymore.

Antoinette V. Franklin

Racism

I was introduced to racism one bright sunny day at the age of three. My family was moving into the house on 852 Gulf Street. It was a nice Spring day. The adults were busy unpacking boxes filled with dishes and clothes. I was the youngest and was told to go out and play since I was getting into everything.

I took my two dollies and my tea set. I found a nice spot beside the wash house under the fig tree. I played and sang a song, roll, roll, your boat gently down the stream until I heard a little voice, there stood a little girl with blonde hair. She asked if she could play? I said yes and gave her one of my dolls and a cup. I told her my name was Antoinette. She replied she was Susie. We played a little while, passing the dolls through the fence.

She stopped and stared at me funny and said, "You are NIGGAR." Her face turned from friendly to anger and she looked at me as if I stank. I had a bath this morning. I didn't know what that word was because I had not heard it before. I stood up and told her to put her hand through the fence. I then bit her and twisted her fingers.

Susie let out a scream that echoed through the neighborhood. She cried and I began to cry. When I turned and saw my family standing near the fig tree. My father, my mother, my great grandmother and my sister had such concern on their faces. Picked me up gently placing me in his arms. He asked "Nette" what happened? I knew I was in trouble, but I told him that she called me a N i g g a r. My father frowned a little but had a tiny smile on his face. At that moment a whited haired white woman began running down the wooden step and grabbed Susie, saying to come into the house. She jerked the little girl's arm and never turned to say she was sorry.

I had both of my dolls and teacups. I never saw the little girl and I didn't go near the fence after that time. The neighborhood had been where many white people were living and since Blacks were moving in, they were moving out. I would play with the Mexican children next door to where the little girl's grandmother lived or played by myself. That is such an ugly word. I always remember how her face looked when she said it.

When I attended Holy Redeemer the sisters of The Holy Family. Sister said a niggar was a low-class person and we were not low-class people. We were taught to love one another and that we were no better than another person.

My Mother's Courage

I experienced racism again when I was seven. My mother was driving on the new freeway IH 35. Mother drove the 57 Ford Fairlane with care. My baby brother was sitting between us, at that time we didn't have seat belts.

There was a car that pulled alongside our car and edged close to the driver's side. I looked at my mother and said, 'Don't look at them." She raised her head high like a queen and kept driving and lifted her head up as if she were a queen.

They were ugly white men, cussing out the window, saying that N word. My mother exited quickly, and I prayed for our safety. The car continued down the freeway. We must teach respect to everyone and put this into practice. The children will take over when we are no longer on the planet and we need to leave a better world for them.

Racism is ugly, damaging, dangerous and frightening. It is time for a change. We have come too far and as John Lewis said, we must speak out about this and vote. Education and tolerance are important for survival. Dr. King and the Freedom Riders did their job and laid the road for us to follow.

I worked for civil service for a total of 37 year and experienced racism daily. First at Kelly AFB then at Lackland AFB. I taught English as a Second Language. One of my students from Senegal stated that his great grandfather often spoke of the people who were stolen from the continent.

The people who were stolen all those years ago were not ignorant people. There was not an ignorant person taken from those shores. The people were taken from their homeland and were scattered across the world.

I was told that the people of Africa would not accept me because of the color of my skin. When I met the students, they accepted me and told me they could see Africa all over me. The sad thing is our people have re-invented the color complex. We are all African American, Black. When the police say, "All you Niggars Get Out of the Car. They will not say the high-yellow or the blue black one. When I was younger, the nuns told us we were not niggers. She said that a niggar was a low-class person and we were not low class.

The time has come to join as one comes together and become one people joined to fight injustice, racism, bigotry, hatred. We need to respect one another for the betterment of our nation. We need to vote the man in charge out and our children, our women and our men. Our children are our future, our elderly our wisdom, our women the backbone and our men our strength.

This is 2020 not 1920, 1930, 1940, 1950, 1960, 1970, 1980, 1990. IT IS A TIME FOR CHANGE. Everyone must get busy, Vote. Remember our ancestors and what has been laid out for achievement and success.

Have The Chickens Come Home To Roost?
June 3, 2020

George Floyd took a knee to his neck for 8 minutes and 46 seconds, while handcuffed, not resisting arrest by white Police Officer Chauvin; and three other officers were there too … watching … gazing.

Gasping helplessly --- George pleaded – "I cannot breathe", "I cannot breathe", …

George whimpered, "MAMA help me, I can't breathe."

A crowd gathered looking on in horror at a modern-day lynching in front of their eyes yelling, pleading with Chauvin "get off 'em!", "he's not a threat!"," get off 'em!", "he's not moving!", "get off his neck!!" "He's not even moving!!", "get off of his neck!!!"

They yelled to the other officers, "Y'all other cop's gonna just stand around and just let 'em kill that man in front of you?!?"

George Floyd with an aching, lonely, whimper took his last breath.

Have the chickens come home to roost?

Chauvin all the while, with his hands stuffed in his pockets, smirk on his face, seemed determined to snuff out a man's life. All the while he was looking casually around as if he knew there would be no retribution for this inhumane action. Without a care, he seemed not bothered at all that he was taking a precious life created by God – a child's father, someone's lover, a big brother. You know, it looked like he was thinking … "hum, what will I have for dinner tonight?" Just wondering, did George Floyd's life mean so little to you Chauvin?

George Floyd is dead. His family is left with the memory of the savage way his life was taken. Burning tears streaming down their faces, a hole in their heart, the only way to release some of the pain is to S-C-R-E-A-M!!! Ohh, My God, my God. And grapple with the realization … he's never … coming … home.

Another black person in America who is part of this horrific fraternity. Yet another countless victim of Police Brutality.

Have the chickens come home to roost?

Rumblings started in Minneapolis and spread quickly to Los Angeles, New York, Dallas and Atlanta all in a matter of a day. They were demanding justice, insisting to be heard with loud and unyielding voices; carrying signs – "No justice – No peace"; "Black Lives Matter, "I Can't Breathe". Those in power seemed to have been caught off guard. Perhaps they were thinking they'll get tired, it's in the middle of a Pandemic; we'll tell them we arrested Chauvin that should quiet them down.

Have the chickens come home to roost?

A fire has been lit across the country; protests popped up across the nation. The demands for Justice has reached out and stretched across the ocean; other countries are joining the protest holding up signs and demanding justice for George Floyd and perhaps for the injustices in their own communities. They are yelling "Black Lives Matter " and " I Can't Breathe" from the United Kingdom to Germany to Canada to New Zealand to Iran to Australia to Amsterdam. Steadfast, proud, smart Black millennials have stood up unafraid and reached their hands out to others. Millennials of all races and backgrounds have joined in solidarity; linking arms with different generations who can no longer stomach the vileness and evilness of another person having their life snatched by those who are sworn to protect and serve. They are demanding justice now. Isn't this remarkable in the face of a pandemic that they have to be heard, throwing caution to the wind, they just can't bear this miscarriage of injustice anymore? Maybe they feel like "we" will all explode, or is it because "we" all are just finding it hard to breathe in this toxic atmosphere?

More than 11,000 protesters have been arrested over nine days of unrest to finally get all four police officers charged in George Floyd's death. Chauvin has been upgraded from 3 rd degree murder to 2nd degree murder. The others finally have been charged with 2nd degree murder and aiding and abetting. Now, that's good right??? Will the rumblings across the country settle down now? Will the marchers put down their signs? Can everything go back to the way it was??? WHY NOT???

LISTEN … Convictions for all of them are needed next.

Read the sign – **No justice – No peace** . Do you know what that really means? No, you say?

Not clear on what that means?? Well, look at the Declaration of Independence "We hold these truths to be self-evident, that all men are created equal, that they are endowed by their Creator with certain unalienable Rights… "[1]

Are we moving toward that change? Well, it's moving too slow. And it's been moving slow for far too long. The pressure has to be kept on. "Power cannot be received without demand".

To those in charge, to those in power - Get it right this time …

Marchers, you're angry, hurt and fed-up … got it! So, vote, **vote, VOTE** and hold them accountable. Know your power! Don't lose your momentum! It's in your hands.

Because … **The chickens have come home to roost.**

Antoinette Franklin

---

[1] Reference: Declaration of Independence (US 1776)

C. E. Lara

The Waterfront ^(c)

I was mesmerized, looking out at the water. The waves, gently flowing in and out. The water seemed to motion peacefully as if trying to provide comfort. I glanced up toward the sky. I saw the full moon showing its reflection on the water. Hearing the lapping sounds of the waves had a soothing, calming effect on me.

I took a deep breath when I heard an interruption. Clearing his throat, he said, "Ahem, excuse me, sorry for the delay. I'm back. May I get your statement now?" Warily turning from such a beautiful view, I exhaled and said, "so, you want me to start from the moment we parked?" He nodded and said, "yes ma'am". A little earlier, he had already made the customary introductions to most of the witnesses. Finally making it around to me, "I'm Officer Jackson" he said in a soothing, tenor voice. I observed him. He held his pad and pen with precision, as if he had been doing his job for several years. Slightly distracted, I noted to myself that he was tall, I'd say about six feet, three inches. "Hmm", I thought, as I eyed him on the sly. Chuckling to myself, I thought, "now, I've had a trying day, but I couldn't help but notice that the officer's uniform was fitting him well. It appeared to me that he probably worked out several times a week. Close-cut, dark brown hair. And no, he didn't throw me a 'Denzel Washington' smile with the whitest teeth. Wow, they're perfectly straight. I bet he wore braces as a kid. Mentally, I thought about my best single girlfriends, who might be a potential match. I hadn't even gotten my list started good when I glanced at his left hand and sighed. "Oh shoot, he's off the market" I thought. I was always on the lookout for potential good match-ups for "my girlfriends."

Anyway, (focus girl I thought to myself). Officer Jackson sat on the hood of his car. I suppose, so he wouldn't have to look down on me and at five feet, five inches tall, and I wouldn't have to strain to look up at him. Then he looked at me with deep, dark brown eyes and politely said, "yes ma'am, you can start at the beginning, it's your story. Let me know what transpired, everything you think that's important. The more detail you provide will help in the long run." I swallowed hard and said, "Okay. Here goes."

"Johnny and I thought we were lucky, blessed, really when we found the last parking spot along the crowded waterfront. From our vantage point, we had a spectacular view. As we looked out from the comfort of the car, the water was glistening. It was an unusually sunny Sunday afternoon. We had just come from church. We felt renewed for the week both in spirit and mind. Thinking back, it was a very spirit-filled service. Almost everyone in our little church felt the 'Holy Ghost" singing praises to the Lord. We both had meetings right after church that ran over schedule. Walking to the car, we looked at each other feeling exhausted. Johnny said, "let's go get something to eat".

We decided to try something different and came to this section of the waterfront, Pier of Délicieux. I looked toward the restaurants, conjuring more pleasant memories. Officer Jackson, "did you know that the pier had just completed an extensive renovation and added several upscale restaurants?" He looked up from his pad and smiled and said "yes, my wife and I just hadn't had an opportunity to come down here yet." I continued on, "well, all of them have received rave reviews by some of the top food critics in town.

Officer Jackson listened with interest to my story, "After Johnny parked his car." I motioned with my head, "see, that light blue Mercedes Benz over there." Then I pointed to the car parked perfectly. "I looked to see how far we were from the restaurant. The restaurant we chose, Seafood Blu, was a good three blocks away. There was some uneven pavement along the way. I thought it might be hard tackling that distance in heels and trying to look chic. It's like my throbbing feet said "pssst, don't even think about it!'" Officer Jackson started smiling, like he was trying to hold back a laugh. I let that slide, thinking about what had happened to me earlier in the evening. I continued on with my story, "Well, I decided it would be best to slip into more comfortable and practical shoes. I quickly pulled off my pretty new cobalt three-inch shoes. They weren't quite broken in anyhow. Ohh, I let my toes stretch, wiggle and get some air before putting on my ole faithful black flats. But for real, I wanted to throw on some jeans instead of keeping on this A-line asymmetrical blue and white dress. I'm just keeping it 100, Officer Jackson! Anyway, Johnny is always the perfect gentleman. He patiently waited for me to change my shoes, powder my nose, and touch-up my lipstick. He got out of the car, briskly walked around to my side, and opened the door for me. He gently, yet firmly took my hand and helped me out of the car. I felt safe. I appreciate it when a man enjoys being a protector without smothering me. You know what I mean Officer Jackson? He flipped over the sheet of paper and said "yes 'mam, I know what you mean."

"Well, Officer Jackson, our afternoon started off delightful. My old faithful flats weren't even hurting my feet! Johnny and I both checked our Fitbit trackers." I turned to him and said "I should hit my goal by the time we get back to the car." He laughed and asked "what's your goal today honey?" I winked and said "it's Sunday, so only 10,000 steps today!" As I navigated the partial cobblestone sidewalk, I thought to myself, "hey, you're pulling it off. You look stylish and you're always a lady". He seemed pleased. We had fun when we were together.

I loved it when he would tenderly squeeze my hand. He had a way of looking loving into my eyes, then giving me an affectionate smile. It was almost as if he were saying "I've got you, don't ever worry." While we were walking to the restaurant, we'd catch glimpses of people smiling at us. Several couples nodded at us as we strolled by. They would say "you two make a lovely couple".

When we arrived at the restaurant, it didn't take long for us to be seated. Delightful aromas of surf and turf and different types of freshly made breads filled the air to give us a warm welcome. We had a delightful lunch and great conversation, so much so that time got away from us. We were there for hours. We got lost in each other's eyes, talking about our plans for the next few days. We didn't hear anything going on around us. As I glanced at my watch I said, "Oh Johnny, wow, look at the time and we both have meetings in the morning!" We were both surprised. Looking around the restaurant, the servers were setting up for dinner. "Bertha, we'd better go", he said. Our server, Nan, whose fiery, red hair was pulled back into a neat ponytail accentuated her oval-shaped face. She seemed to have as many freckles as there are stars in the sky. Nan said "I'll be right back with you", as she briskly walked by. Her bubbly personality had lasted throughout our stay. Soon she came back to our table smiling. "Did you two have a good time?" Beaming Johnny said, "Yes we most certainly did". He paid Nan, left her a generous tip; and we hurried out the door.

Looking back now, I think if we hadn't been in such a rush to get to the car, we would have been more attentive. But we were so giddy, so new in love. We were looking at each other, laughing, just having a good time. Perhaps we may have "kept our head on a swivel" as my daddy used to warn me. As Johnny and I approached the car, it was getting dusky, the golden hue of the sun had just started to fade. I remember turning to Johnny, saying "sweetie, look at the beautiful sunset." We paused, he gazed out taking it in and he said: "yes baby, it's stunning, just like you."

Then it seemed like it was out of some crazy movie. This tall, husky guy sprang up from around one of the parked cars. He had a knife pointed at us. It was more at me. His attention was focused toward me. His blue eyes fixated and locked on mine. He turned his square-shaped face ever so slightly toward my cheek. Whispering menacingly, so close to my ear that I could feel his hot breath. He demanded with an ever so slight lisp "give me your purse". His voice, although in a whisper was so stern, it frightened me to the core of my stomach. We were startled. We both saw the reflection of the light on the knife from the light post. My eyes got big. Then, he tried to yank my purse, but I had it across my shoulder and body. As he yanked my purse, my heart was pounding hard … pounding harder, my head was spinning. I started yelling – NOoooOO!! I can remember, I lost my balance and fell forward. The next thing I remember is falling on him and hearing a big - blob! My legs were sprawled up in the air --- KICKING! Back and forth so fast! KICKING!! Back and forth!! I was YELLING – "JESUS! JESUS – HELP ME JESUSSS!!"

It seemed as if this was all happening in slow motion and lasting forever. Surely it was only a matter of seconds. I don't know for sure, but I started thinking "What is happening!" AND then, I realized "Girl YOUR LEGS ARE UP IN THE AIR KICKING!!" *(Then "poof" out of nowhere a particular thought popped into my mind from when I was a little girl, my Mama saying:*

"make sure you always put on nice, clean underwear just in case you're ever in an accident" … well mentally, I started to quickly do a checklist in my head … yep, underwear is good - check. Now try to get your legs DOWN!!). I started desperately struggling, squirming trying to get my dress from around my waist to at least my thighs. Then, I started working my dress down to my knees. Well, dear God, I thought, there goes looking lady like! Like a blink of an eye, my man was like Superman! No … no, I'd say he was more spot-on like Black Panther! Well, he pulled me up and kicked that thug right in his groin. The guy doubled over in pain and gave out a piercing howl "Owww! Man-n-n!" Johnny turned to pick me up and said, "baby, you alright?"

Oh, my goodness, out of nowhere, it seemed as if people crowded around that ole dirty goon so he couldn't go anywhere. Truth be told, he was still doubled over. Nope, I don't think he was able to go anywhere! The next thing, I heard sirens interrupting the murmuring of the crowd. I saw the lights flashing on and off of the faces of the people standing around. And then, Officer Jackson, you showed up. This guy here, officer, my man, well he's my hero." I took a long, deep breath and let it out slowly before saying, "now, you can get his version of what happened." I smiled, and beamed proudly at Johnny. I watched as he started telling his version to Officer Jackson.

I started thinking about how blessed Johnny and I had been on the waterfront. Neither of us had received one scratch from that guy's knife! I wasn't hurt after falling on the mugger. Wowzers, I just had a flashback! I hope I don't wind up on someone's social media post. Oh, my goodness, showing me falling on that thug with my legs flailing around in the air. Embarrassing! I shuddered at the thought. I had to chuckle a bit at the notion … but just a bit.

I looked at my watch, then at Johnny. He and Officer Jackson were just about to finish up. It was getting late. As if he were continuing to protect me. Johnny came over and took my hand, squeezed it lovingly. He bent down, tenderly kissing me on my lips. "How are you holding up, sweetheart?" He asked and I seemed to melt. Trying to hold back tears now. Oh, I welcomed his strong arms around me as he hugged me. I whispered, "good, because you're here. Thanks for having my back sweetie." He smiled and said, "I consider it a pleasure for my queen."

Attempting to lighten the mood, he said, "I can hardly wait to see what excitement awaits when I pick you up next weekend." I smiled and said, "Right now, as for me, well, I could use a cup of coffee to settle my nerves! I've got a meeting in the morning." We held hands, laughed, and walked toward the car. What an experience on the waterfront!

C. E. Lara

You Had No Right [©]
October 14, 2020

Her beautiful, soulful eyes staring back at me, concealing many chapters of her life's story.

On television I see "breaking news", they flash a picture of her face … Oh God, not again!

On magazine covers, captivatingly beautiful eyes follow me until I am compelled to pick up the magazine and read her story.

Once again, I am pained, shocked by how her life was taken.

Sometimes, I will walk down a crowded street to look at her mural.

Her eyes seem to speak out to me.

So much potential. Forever unfulfilled.

I wonder …

Who would she have become?
What would she have accomplished?
I don't know. No one ever will … now.

A life unfulfilled because someone ferociously decided she had no worth. No value. And it seems without as much forethought of thumping a cigarette butt to the ground and stepping on it … he snuffed out all her fire and energy. He extracted the multiple pieces of her God-given kaleidoscope that were sweet, saucy, feisty, and more … that made her unique.

Antoinette Franklin

WHETHER …

- He busted into her home with a no-knock warrant, or;
- She was kidnapped from Ft. Hood Military Base, or;
- She died in custody – *questionably* – alone in a jail cell, or;
- She was snatched off the street;

He stole her life! Her potential, her future, her decisions.
It was HERS!

Whatever she would have become. Whatever path she would have chosen.

Whatever she would have done with her life - **it was hers.**

Now it is gone — forever.

YOU HAD NO RIGHT TO TAKE IT FROM HER!

When I hear her story or see her eyes; there is an overwhelming sense of sadness.

Another precious life interrupted in such a vile way.

I say her name. Again … and again.

And each time …

I think about her family, being told she's gone. Inconsolable, with uncontrollable tears. Yelling, screaming, crying out … "NO-o-o!!" "MY BABY." "MIJA." It is a nightmare. Resolute to plead with God in Heaven for strength to carry on … because … she is gone.

Their hearts are aching. Will their tears, pain, disbelief of this nightmare ever stop? Will their heart ever stop hurting? I see them crying out, to God as they look to heaven for help. Slowly, the gut-wrenching reality sinks in.

Memories are all that they have left now. This is not fair. This is not right.

Family. Friends. Even strangers … join in and we will say her name and think about her.

In many cases, she was already a productive member of her community. I wonder, what else would she have contributed to her community or society-at-large? Whether significant, big or small. It doesn't matter really; it was her life and her right to live it. It was her right to - just be able to BREATHE!

This is a travesty and should be crushing to our human spirit - shouldn't it?

Why does this list of women continue to grow?

STOP THIS Madness!

Don't let her death be in vain.

We must stay vigilant. We have to stay aware. Take action.

It is pivotal to continue voting, marching, writing and speaking out. We need to be involved, get involved, and stay involved. No one else should succumb to this type of tragic death. Everyone can do something. Everyone … you are not too young; you are never too old … activate your voice! Let the power of your voice be heard!

I implore you to join hands across the aisle with people of different colors, ethnicities, genders, religions … work together to create a more humane society, don't stop. There's still so much more to do.

My heart aches because of the ever-growing tragic list of beautiful, smart, feisty, daughters, sisters, nieces, granddaughters, friends whose potential; whose lives were cut short.

I hope not … but …

Next time it might hit closer to your "home".

She may be your little girl … your daughter.

She could even be your beloved little sister or the big sister. You know, the one you've always looked up to.

Maybe next - your niece or even your "grandbaby" – Sweet little girl.

She could even be your friend … your best friend.

She might even be You.

SAY. HER. NAME.

The light has been turned off on so many … TOO MANY.

YOU WILL NOT BE FORGOTTEN.

I honor your life, all that you were, and could have been. Gone too soon:

- Breonna Taylor – killed March 13, 2020
- Private First-Class Officer Vanessa Guillen – killed/disappeared April 22, 2020
- Atatiana K. Jefferson – killed October 2019
- Sandra Bland – killed July 2015
- Natasha McKenna – killed February 2015
- Alexia Christian – killed 2015
- Meagan Hockaday – killed 2015
- Mya Hall – killed 2015
- Janisha Fonville – killed 2015
- Gabriella Nevarez – killed 2014
- Aura Rosser – killed 2014
- Michelle Cousteau – killed August 2014
- Tanisha Anderson – killed 2014

Someone loved her. Someone cared.
SAY HER NAME!

Making A Jewel

Antoinette V. Franklin

My Favorite Library Story - I

A wonderful library patron told me this story about a conversation with former librarian Ms. Addie Armstrong. Mr. Nathaniel Bridges is an avid Lakers basketball fan and one of the games between the San Antonio Spurs and the Los Angeles Lakers was being played in San Antonio. Mr. Bridges was visiting the Carver library. Ms. Armstrong was a devoted Spurs fan and she told Mr. Bridges he could not wear that team tee shirt in the library. Mr. Bridges was shocked but played it off not getting upset but laughing.

(Story told by Nathaniel Bridges)

Antoinette V. Franklin

My Favorite Library Story - II

My father would take me to the downtown public library on Saturdays every two weeks. He would tell me he was going to circle the block and that should be about 15 minutes. He did this so he would not have to park. There were times we would ride the bus and go to the library or to the Cameo to the movie, but on days when he worked on weekends we went to the library. I would enter the library and go downstairs. That was where the books I wanted to read were held.

I read about George Washington Carver and Mary Mcleod Bethune and many others. I liked Nancy Drew also. I always enjoyed going to the library and reading is my favorite thing to do. I loved books and reading. My mother told me I couldn't bring the book to the table because she wanted to see my pretty face.

I have lived in San Antonio all my life except for one year when I lived in Austin. I came back to help my mother after my father had a stroke. When I had my daughter, Alexis, I bought a home on the east side down the street from my family's home. Our special time together was to go to the Carver library. She would get one a book and lay on the floor. I would get one as well and we would spend time in the library. A dear friend told me loved the east side and could not leave his home. The east side gets a bad reputation, but it is a great place to live, grow up and call home.

There are many good people living here and there are children to be educated here.

My Favorite Library Story - III

There is so much history, and it is growing and changing for the better. There are wonderful memories I share with people of my upbringing. It is sad when I hear people talk unfavorably about San Antonio, it is not anything to do and it is not progressive as some other cities. Well you make the best of where you have been planted and do the best. There are terrific places to visit and learn about. The library offers this information for free. Get your library card and take the journey.

"Learn Something New Every Day" My mother, Ruth Lara Franklin would always say. We must pass positive things to our children to encourage them to be the best. "Do Right" were her wisdom words that had been passed down from Phyllis Wheatley High School Principal Mr. S. J. Sutton. My mother graduated from Phillis Wheatley High School in 1939. My entire family, my aunts, uncles, and cousins attended this school and graduated. There were many streets named after famous Black people who made a difference on the east side. Ira Aldridge (African American actor), Roberson after African American actor Paul Roberson and Gable Street was once Harrison named after Fannie Lou Harrison. It is good to know your history. The Sutton family were wonderful people who made a difference on the east side. There were Negro owned businesses on Commerce St. E. Houston Street. The people on the east side took pride in the community and supported each other. I have a home on the east side down the street from where I grew up and I support activities and children in various schools on the east side.

There were Black cab companies that helped the citizens to get around. These cabs were: Bellinger, Hartfield, and the Montgomery families. The Sutton family were people who made a difference in the community. Mr. S. J. Sutton was the principal of Phillis Wheatley High School and taught the students to "Do Right." One of his sons, Percy Sutton was a Tuskegee Airman and later became a civil rights leader and was lawyer for Malcom X His brother Garlington Jerome, G. J. Sutton became the first Black Texas elected official. A building bearing his name was torn down in 2019. Sutton and Sutton were one of the funeral homes. The Collins family had the Collins Funeral home and the Lewis family had one of the other funeral homes. There was another funeral home on the west side, but most of the black businesses were on the east side. There was a funeral home owned by Blacks on the west side.

Holy Redeemer Catholic School was the black school along with St. Peter Claver. Holy Redeemer didn't have a large library, but I made use of what was there. An assortment of books about George Washington Carver, Booker T. Washington, Mary McCloud Bethune, President George and Martha Washington, John Adams Abigail Adams, Florence Nightingale, Madame Curie, Mozart, and Beethoven. I loved mysteries and read Sherlock Holmes and Agatha Christie. I was excited when the library added new books. When I entered St Gerard high school after integration, I joined the library club. I love books and reading.

Antoinette V. Franklin

My Favorite Library Story - IV

Another wonderful moment was when Mr. Author B. Winn was playing for a Christmas party with a group of poets, Debra F. Medows, Isaac Green and Abram Emerson. Mr. Arthur Winn played back up base and was reading. There were three little children sitting Indian style, and each child was sucking their thumbs, the little brother was looking up at the ceiling. I thought he wasn't paying attention. The other sister asked Mr. Winn, Can't you play no Blues? He was playing Jingle Bells. He laughed and said, "Yes Baby, I can play some blues."

The program ended and the children ate cookies, drank juice, and were given a book. I noticed the same little boy that had been sucking his thumb with his sisters coming toward me. He looked very nervous. I stopped, leaned down toward him, so maybe he would not be afraid, and I smiled. He said, "Thank-you for those beautiful words." I was so touched, and, on that day, I received a Million Dollars from his smile and his sincere words. I learned to not take anything for granted. I had thought before the child was not listening. The little boy was listening and had enjoyed the program.

C. E. Lara

My Favorite Library Story
My Library Memories

I remember going to the library with my Mom (I called her Mommy then) at a young age, even before enrolling into elementary school. We held hands walking into, what seemed to me, a gigantic building. I would look all around. Up and down the aisles my curious, excited eyes would dart. To my young eyes, it seemed like so many books in all sizes and shapes! And those books seemed as if they would go on and on for miles … oh what fun and delight!

I loved being with my Mommy anytime. But the library was such an adventure. The way she would read the books to me, the stories would come alive; we would be transported anywhere. She could read stories with such great expressions. She would take on voices of the characters and I could almost see and feel them in my mind's eye! An extra treat would be family time when my Mommy and my maternal grandmother (I called her Mula) would each take turns to read stories … that was so much fun! Then, when I learned to read, we each took our turn. I learned to read with expression. That was the educator in my Mom; teaching and passing down a family tradition.

Years later, I would venture to the library with my class or either on my own. I was so excited when I was able to get my library card. Having a library card, what a responsibility! I still remember helpful librarians, the process of checking out books and returning them.

A fond memory is my elementary teacher reading to our class. I remember being so enthralled with her delivery of *Charlotte's Web* by E. B. White that I had to go to the library to read it again for myself. When I got a little older, I discovered one of my favorite's poets Langston Hughes. His book, The Panther and the Lash, I read and re-read this book many times. Another poet, James Weldon Johnson, in my opinion, his poem "The Creation" is magnificent. I recall memorizing this poem in high school; for various competitions and won. Another book I recall as a reading assignment in high school is, *1984* by George Orwell, wow … who knew what a reference it would have today. I have so many more fond memories of Carver Branch Library that helped me grow and thrive. I am so glad Carver Branch and the Main Library was there for me with books and helpful librarians. I hope that both will be around for generations to come.

Linda Oliver

Library is my holy home

I fell in love with God and life…words & books … The library is my holy home…living in expectation is new for me…living has been the way to go for me…

Don Mahis

The Trouble with Reading

The Bookmobile used to visit my neighborhood when I was in junior high school. I was interested in mysteries and found a new book. *"13 Ways to Kill a Man"* (1965, edited by Basil Davenport) in this little library on wheels. This anthology of short stories was an easy read; I finished it within days.

The first story, *"The Candidate "* by Henry Slesar, was a perfect crime. A victim was informed that hundreds of people were wishing him dead. Such knowledge was apparently enough to send a man to the grave.

"Lamb to the Slaughter" was my introduction to Roland Dahl, it was another rate of a perfect crime. The wife bludgeons her husband her husband to death with a frozen leg of lamb—then serves the murder weapon to the investing officers. Some crimes are discovered, such as the strangling murder (The Turn of the Tide by C. S. Forester) and the burning death *("Hop Frog "* by Edgar Allan Poe), but others keep the reader intrigued until the end.

The story of death by stabbing is particularly ingenious. "The Tea Leaf," by Edgar Jepson and Robert Eustace, dagger is formed from a dozen carbon dioxide and conveyed in a thermos into a sauna. Because the murder weapon turns to vapor as it melts, no one suspects the culprit.

Other murders are committed by shooting, poison, starvation, animals, explosion, vehicle, and electrocution. But the real crime of this book is the trouble I got into for checking it out.

Judging from the title, my mother thought I was doing research to kill someone. And she voiced her concerns to the authorities'. I was interrogated by my teacher. The librarian in the bookmobile revoked my library card.

I felt like a criminal.

La Juana (LJ) Chambers Lawson

COVID-19

I am writing this in San Antonio, Texas on Tuesday, September 22, 2020. To date, the globally destructive and life-altering COVID-19 pandemic has been cited in more than 967,000 deaths worldwide and 203,000 deaths in the United States. For clarification, this data is cited by a (relatively reliable) federal/national agency - the Center for Disease Control (CDC). Epidemiologists throughout the nation have been sharing an interesting fact as it relates to the death toll of the coronavirus global public health pandemic. And that is that the disease - COVID-19 - that is caused by a coronavirus known globally as SARS-CoV-2 disproportionately kills Black and brown people. More specifically, COVID-19 is outright lethal for Black and brown people with pre-existing cardiac and/or respiratory conditions. We (as a world of nations and citizens) have been losing family and friends with nonfatal pre-existing conditions like asthma, diabetes, and heart disease who would have undoubtedly still been living had it not been for COVID-19. Their deaths were entirely preventable.

Personally, I have lost dozens of family and friends to COVID-19. I blame no particular persons for their deaths because I do not adhere to the great man theory of leadership that so many interpret and perpetuate in their (really, lack of) circumspect decision-making. The great man theory of leadership holds that some people are born with the necessary attributes that set them apart from others and that these traits are responsible for their assuming positions of positions and authority. I am here to tell you that this paternalistic and unempowering perspective of who is a leader versus who is not is disgustingly deterministic and disemboweling. In reality, I believe and want others to believe that we are all naturally born leaders who, under differing circumstances, come into and out of roles that we assume through appointment, election, or force at consequence to our capacity, intention(s), as well as health and wellness at particular points in our lifetimes. When decisions are made that do not serve our own rational interest, the onus is us to correct or demand what we think is better or what we believe serves our interest(s). No matter the governing structure or societal norms that may be in place, we are individually responsible to ourselves, our families, and our communities. Picture Hobbes' Leviathan. The monster and his dominion are indistinguishable from the individuals who lend to him his influence and power. All the while, the leader lies docile as the individuals lend her only their woes, hopes, and unrealized dreams. We are the monsters that march us to our ruinous oblivion.

The family and friends that we have lost to COVID-19 should awaken us all to the very real fact that the chickens have come home to roost. That is, the comfort that some of us have enjoyed for as long as my memory serves me has utterly blinded, distracted, and in most cases outright slaughtered the majority of us.

Our silence cannot protect us.

Comfort for the majority of us has been and is unattainable.

The world that colonists have constructed and stratified for their tyrannistic gain now has more reward than associated risks than ever before. Our docility is our ruin.

Antoinette V. Franklin

Making a Jewel

Reference

Making a Jewel
How I Got Over
Authors Bios of Members

Beatrice Anderson Carver Literary Arts Society Anthology 2010, Set Your Compass to the Stars. Imagination 2019.

Grace Banks retired office manager. Member of the Carver Literary Arts Society. Published in Set Your Compass to the Stars and Imagination 2018.

Haywood Bethel poet, author, humor and motivational speaker.

George Bussey retired educator from Lackland AFB. Former native of New York. Resides in St. Lucia, Florida. Published in Set Your Compass to the Stars and Imagination 2018.

Florine Davis singer, actress, composer. Member of Carver Literary Arts Society.

Aaron Doyle Carver Literary Arts Society member.

Sandra Fergins poet, actress, author. Worked with Hornsby Entertainment.

Antoinette V. Franklin received the Arts and Letters Award from San Antonio Public Library 2019. Creative Writing Instructor at Carver Library since 2008. Retired ESL Instructor from Lackland AFB. BA 1978 University of Incarnate Word, MA Management Webster University 1990, MA Ed. University of the Incarnate Word 1998. PhD student, Poet, Author, Educator.

Tia Gibson Monster Moms coordinator, member of Carver Literary Arts Society.

D. l. Grant Carver Library Branch Manager. PhD 2020. Published in Carver Literary Arts Society 2010 and A Hundred Dollar Bet.

Joanna Hargrove Carver Literary Arts Society member. Native of New York. Mother, grandmother, newly graduated minister 2019.

Lou Hopson Retired Army Registered Nurse, Member Delta Sigma Theta Sorority. Community Activist for disadvantaged, displaced people. Member of Carver Literary Arts Society.

Tom Howie artist artwork has appeared in Imagination Carver Literary Arts Society 2019, member of Carver Arts Society.

C. E. Lara native of San Antonio, TX. Earned MBA from California State University, Los Angeles and BBA from Our Lady of the Lake. Business professional.

Frances Philips Lee writer and teacher at the young age of 90 year of wisdom.

Linda Oliver native of San Antonio, now resides in Arizona. Actress, writer. Published in Set your Compass to the Stars.

Don Mathis is editor and publisher of "The Fourteen Percenter" a newsletter for noncustodial parents, Don is a poet, journalist, a concerned father, and loving grandfather. Though this family resides hours apart they always remain close to one another's heart.

Sulema Mendoza poet, community activist.

Andrea Sanderson "Vocab' San Antonio first African American Poet Laureate 2020-2022 is a San Antonio native that's been performing for over twenty years. She has served as a Teaching Artist for Gemini Ink since 2009. Sanderson is the winner of the 2019 *People's Choice Award* Luminaria Artist Foundation, and a 2020 recipient of the Friends of San Antonio Public Library *Arts and Letters Award* . Her debut book is entitled: *She Lives in Music,* Flower Song Press 2020. Her album, *She Tastes like Music* is available on all music streaming platforms. On April 1st 2020, Andrea became the first African American, Poet Laureate of San Antonio 2020-2023. www.andreavocabsanderson.com IG: Vocabulous

Courtney Smith Carver Literary Arts Society assistant editor, ESL instructor at Lackland AFB.

La Juana (LJ) Chambers Lawson author of A Project Manager's Guide to Grant Writing, Owner and Principal Consultant of Tacit Growth Strategies, LLC in San Antonio, TX. She is a Lecturer at Our Lady of the Lake University and an Instructor of Project Management at the University of the Incarnate Word. Earned a MPA and BA from Virginia Commonwealth University.

April Poetry Contest 2020
Poetry Contest

1 st prize $20.00 Don Mathis
2 nd prize $15.00 Sandra Fergins
3 rd prize $10.00 Beatrice Anderson
Honorable Mention George Bussey

Printed in the United States
by Baker & Taylor Publisher Services